CODE NAME: PAPA

ALIYAH BURKE

Entangled Publishing, LLC
2614 South Timberline Road
Suite 109
Fort Collins, CO 80525
Visit our website at www.entangledpublishing.com.

Select Suspense is an imprint of Entangled Publishing, LLC.

Edited by Robin Haseltine
Cover design by Heather Howland
Cover art by iStock

Manufactured in the United States of America

First Edition July 2015

To my readers, thanks for coming along on another journey. To those who accept the mantle of parenthood when it's thrust upon them even if they find out years later. To DH, thanks for always having my back no matter what. And last, yet never least, to the men and women who sacrifice so much to serve their country so I can remain safe, God bless and thank you!

Chapter One

"Why don't you tell me what the fuck was so important I had to leave my post, risk my cover, not to mention the op, only to drive like crazy for almost three hundred miles to this place. Wherever it is." Sure, he had GPS, but he was pissed. The phone to his ear, he waited impatiently for the man on the other end to answer him.

Beckett Hanson, a veteran agent of a secret government group called EGIS—they dealt in things most others couldn't or *wouldn't* do to keep, not just the country, but the world safe—sat in the parked truck, avoiding the oppressive sun the best he could. This older vehicle had no air-conditioning to help combat the desert heat, but at least the flowing air had cooled him while he'd been driving. Now, parked near the corner of a dingy police station, in this puny no-name town with stagnant air lingering around, the sweat, again, trailed down his back.

He scratched with frustration at the three days' worth of growth on his face and then drummed his fingers along his thigh and glared out the window.

"You're there for an intercept and retrieval," his boss finally admitted.

Beckett frowned, lips flattening. Intercept? Retrieval? "Both? In the middle of an op? Who the hell am I getting, Michael?"

He'd never been pulled from an op before to get someone.

"Once you're inside you'll get it. Get in. Get out. Get back. ASAP. Whatever you do, make sure this person *remains* in *your* custody. They're expecting someone but not you. The person you're replacing has been detained slightly."

Great. "Name?" They'd always told him that before—if the information had been gathered.

The front door burst open and two men stumbled through, one clutching his nose, the other his groin. Jesus, what was going on in there? The day was going to hell. Acquiring someone as an intercept meant others would be after him. Couple that with a prisoner, and this potentially volatile situation would be even more so.

"Go." The call ended.

With a curse, he looked at the phone and then shoved it in his pocket. Readjusting his ball cap a bit lower over his sunglasses, he hopped out and strode to the building. In all his years as an operative, he'd never had such an odd assignment. And he'd been on some weird ones.

He was grateful for his firearm and the backup on his ankle. Danger always lurked when impersonating a member of the local law. However, the situation was worse when you had no clue whom you were supposed to be getting. At least from the size of the building, he bet there weren't that many prisoners inside. In addition, if they were expecting a pickup, the prisoner should be ready. Hopefully, the description of the man supposed to be picking up the prisoner wasn't stated.

Opening the station's door, he muttered as he walked into a wall of heated air, this time combined with the pungent stench of unwashed bodies. He should have expected there would be no respite from the heat in here.

The next second, all thoughts of the heat vanished. At least the kind from the sun. A very loud and unfortunately familiar voice rang out with explicit threats to a certain part of male anatomy.

Beckett's steps faltered until he managed to shove the past where the voice had come from—behind him. He fisted his hands briefly, nails biting into his palms. Blinking as his eyes adjusted, he scanned the room. Two cops, both sporting serious scowls, and the person he knew was his retrieval. His heart thudded.

After all this time…now, *now* she showed back up in his life? She looked less than thrilled to see him. Not that it shut her up.

"Damn you!" she screamed, jerking against the bench to which they'd cuffed her. "Let me go!"

How'd Bogie put it? *Of all the gin joints in all the towns in all the world, she…*

It took all he had not to stare at her and memorize every inch. Her. Indigo Grey. At one time his partner—in more ways than one—until she'd vanished. Off the grid. Gone dark. Now, almost eight years later, here she was. As beautiful as the day she'd left his life. Perhaps more so. Smooth dark skin, full lips, and her brown eyes that currently flashed with anger.

"I'm here for the prisoner," he stated once he reached the counter.

How the hell had Michael found her out in this no-man's land? Why had he even been looking for her? What the hell had *she* done to get herself tossed into this place?

He was going to kill his boss.

On the corner of one desk, an old oscillating fan rattled and shook, doing what it could to stir the air, which wasn't much. The officer facing him was a large man, sweaty, and in an obvious bad mood.

"Took you long enough."

The officer ran his gaze up and down him, as if checking for something, and yet at the same time it was an automatic action. He didn't blame him. How often did something happen in this speck on the map?

Beckett didn't move while the man looked. He wore jeans and a T-shirt, no different from a lot of the law around here. There was no hiding the sidearm he wore, and he didn't attempt to. Sure, he looked a bit rough, but, damn it all, it wasn't as if he'd had time for a shave.

Despite the years and the way she'd disappeared on him, there was a part of him—a part he tried to forget—that would always need to protect her.

The man yelled, "Shut up, bitch!" in Spanish and then shook his head. Beckett refused to show emotion.

"You may want to gag her. She's not shut up since they brought her in two days ago. It was quiet until the bitch woke up. But ever since then…this."

Two days? In this hole?

Beckett gave a lewd smirk. "I may. Or toss her in the back of the truck so I don't have to listen to her mouth. I'm sure it could be put to better use."

The man grinned. Without looking, Beckett could feel her daggerlike stare boring into him. The other cop unhooked her from the bench, cuffed her hands together, and shoved her in Beckett's direction. Taking a deep breath, he grabbed her arm. Familiar sparks shot through him at the simple touch.

"Gentlemen." He propelled her to the door, needing to get her out and demand answers.

"Let me go, you bastard!" She jerked against him.

"Walk," he barked, pushing them out once again into the relentless sun. His fingertips dug into her arm.

He did his best not to focus on her smooth, dark skin, but he couldn't quite seem to manage. He knew every inch, every *single* inch of her body. Where her birthmark was. Where she was ticklish and, most importantly, how her large brown eyes darkened to melted dark chocolate during an orgasm. The rasp of her voice as she screamed his name in pleasure.

Shit. Now was so not the time for this.

"You have no right." She increased her struggling, drawing the attention of the two men who'd left before he'd entered. Not what they needed.

"Stop it."

"Go to hell!" She jammed her foot down on his instep and broke to the right.

Damn, that hurt.

He grabbed her, spun her around the corner into the wall, and slammed his mouth over hers with a growl. It was the only way he knew to shut her up—well, not the *only* way, but it sure as hell was the first one he thought of. Her hands, cuffed as they were behind her, thrust her breasts into him. He relished the feel of her against him again. Memories swarmed along with her taste, and it reminded him where they were. Tearing free, he stared into her eyes. Anger and desire sparked there.

"Shut your mouth and let's get out of here."

"Fuck you."

A secure grip on her, he propelled her to his truck, a sardonic grin firmly in place. "Been there. Done that. I'm sure you remember *all* those times."

She stiffened but snapped her mouth shut. Once in the truck, he wasted no time getting them out of there. Indigo didn't move, just sat as close to the door as she could.

"Why did they arrest you?"

Nothing.

He tried again. "Where've you been?"

Crickets.

His cell buzzed, and he readjusted to answer it. "What?"

"You'd better be on your way from there." *Michael.*

"Thanks for telling me. Why are we picking *her* up?" Beckett did his best to sound pissed for no other reason than she was the retrieval he didn't want to do. It had nothing to do with his feelings for her and how he'd believed his heart torn out when she vanished. Right, *nothing* at all to do with that. At all.

"Is she with you?"

"Passenger seat. Answer me."

"Orders go from me to you, not the other way. Bring her in."

He bit back his instinctive rumble of displeasure. "Why her?"

"Just get her here. I'll explain then. How long before you get back?"

Beckett glanced at his watch. "Five to six hours. It's almost three hundred miles and a detour— Shit!"

He slammed on the brakes, the truck fishtailing the moment it hit the shoulder. Dropping the phone, he shut off the engine, jumping out before the vehicle had come to a complete stop.

"Damn it, Indigo!"

She'd leaped from the truck and run full out in the other direction.

Silver glinted in the sun, and he swore again, realizing she'd picked her cuffs. Moreover, she could run. He couldn't help but admire her long, dark, toned legs as they carried her away. Pouring on the speed, he closed the distance, cursing the heat, the fates that had tossed them back together, and his attraction, which apparently continued to run hot and heavy for her.

He didn't give her a chance to slow, just tackled her to the ground. They hit hard, skidding along the fiery ground. She grunted despite his attempt to take the brunt of the fall. Immediately, she fought him, and they ended up face-to-face.

"Would you hold still," he hissed. Tears blurred his eyes from a direct hit she landed.

Pinned beneath him, she lay unmoving. Her chest heaved, and he could feel the powerful beat of her heart through the thin cotton tee she wore. Rising up, he stared into her eyes. A sucker punch to his gut, seeing her so close, sweaty, and breathing hard.

There were times when life just wasn't fair at all. This, right here, would be one of them.

Her eyes however, told a different story. This woman wasn't running from him for any other reason than fear and desperation. But of what? Or whom was she running from? Surely, she knew he wouldn't hurt her. Not really.

The second he relaxed, she moved, nearly succeeding in bucking him off. Then she went for his gun and shit got serious fast.

She might look the same, but no way this was the woman who'd once shared his bed or protected his back. Securing her hands above her head with his, he leaned over her.

"Christ, Indigo. Knock it off. It's just too goddamn hot for this." He cuffed her again and hauled her to her feet. "Walk nicely or I'll toss your ass over my shoulder."

Covered in dirt, blood, and sweat, she glared sideways at him, but remained quiet. He didn't care. He wasn't exactly happy right now, either. Drenched with perspiration, filthy, and seeing stars after the all-too-direct hit from her knee to his privates.

Even so, he wasn't the least bit surprised when she made another attempt to get away. He barely slowed, just hefted her and tossed her over his shoulder like a sack of wheat. With a firm smack on her ass, he marched back to the truck, his mood sinking like a lead balloon with each step.

"Sit," he barked once they reached the vehicle, and he set her down.

She did, her expression mutinous. He stared at her and did a double take; faint bruising on her skin bothered him—she didn't bruise easily—as well as blood from numerous cuts and scrapes. No doubt accumulated when she'd thrown herself from the truck while it was moving. Behind her on the floor, his phone rang.

"Hello, Indigo." He thought he'd try a different tactic. Didn't work—she said nothing. He stared at her before taking her out of the vehicle and handcuffing her to him. "Let's go." He got back in, first this time, and pulled her along. "Shut the door." An order he had to repeat twice more.

Starting the engine, he picked up his phone and called Michael back.

"What the fuck happened?" the man demanded.

"She bolted."

"You let her get away?"

Okay, that was plain insulting. He reached for the shifter, only to pause. "Hang on."

Phone on the dash, he dug for his handcuff key and separated them. He didn't need her going for the gears and causing him to crash. Leaning close, he hooked her to the oh-shit bar, so both her hands were above her head. He took one more hungry perusal of her form.

"Kick me, and I'll cuff your feet, too," he vowed.

She turned her head and stared outside. He got them back on the road and picked up his phone.

"No, I didn't *let* her get away."

"Then what happened?"

"She jackrabbited. Jumped from a moving vehicle, that's what. I don't think she wants to come in." He rolled his shoulders to loosen up the increasing tension in them.

"Tough. Get her here. Moreover, get off that road. By now, they'll know you weren't the one supposed to pick her up." *Click.* Michael was gone.

Beckett tossed his phone down and glanced at his passenger. A trickle of blood trailed down from her temple to her jaw. He had to get her some medical attention. Heeding Michael's warning, he got them off the main road and onto something smaller. Not that there were many choices.

Two hours later, without a single word spoken between them, he pulled into the lot of a run-down motel.

"Stay here." She didn't look at him. "I mean it, Indigo. You run, and things between us will get ugly. I want to get cleaned up and get some answers."

He hurried in and paid cash for the unit farthest from the office and dashed back out. Relief filled him when he saw her. He grabbed his bag from behind the seat and undid her, then escorted her to the door.

The room, while small, had a surprisingly clean look. Wasn't the Ritz, but it would do fine. They'd been in worse. Been in better, too. Her arm still secure in his hand, he checked the entire room. Satisfied she couldn't escape via the bathroom, he pushed her there.

"Shower." He kept his order brusque.

He went to his pack and dug out a clean shirt, then went back to the bathroom door. A solitary knock and he opened it, hung the shirt over the edge of the sink, and left her alone.

With a weary groan, he sank on the lone bed and placed his head in his hands. His ex-partner and ex-lover—who'd bolted on him—just on the other side of that door, stripping naked and showering. What sweet hell had he stumbled into?

• • •

Indigo Grey shook with numerous emotions as she reached in and turned on the shower. She wanted to run, to flee, and she gulped down breaths to stay quiet. One thought ran through her mind: *get Sean back.* However, that single mantra now had a companion—*Beckett Hanson.*

Lord, he looked so good. Hard bodied and capable. The years had been kind to him. His luxurious dark brown hair, offset by incredibly intense cobalt-blue eyes and thick eyelashes, reminded her of all those stolen moments they'd shared.

What had brought EGIS in on this? And why had they come for her? Sure, she'd gone dark, but it seemed highly unlikely they would have caught up with her in the remote jail she'd landed in. She'd worked for them for years and had partnered with Beckett for many of those. Releasing a sharp breath, she shook her head. That had been so long ago; it didn't bode well for her to be in his clutches. And not just Beckett's, but those of EGIS.

She took her few personal items from her pocket and set them on the sink by the dark blue shirt he'd placed there. At the last minute, she remembered to toe off her shoes. She had no socks and no idea where they'd gone. Then she walked into the streaming water, clothes and all.

Indigo hissed in pain as the water pelted her exposed and peeled raw skin. Hands braced along the tiles, she dropped her head and allowed it to cascade down over her. Her energy was gone, options about the same. Nevertheless, she couldn't give up; she *wouldn't* give up. She could steal a car and get back to Puebla. And some money, she'd need money. She didn't even know where the fuck she was, but she was sure it wasn't near where she needed to be.

She slowly lifted her face and stepped out of the stream. Removing her clothing, she used the soap and water to clean those best she could, then washed herself.

Think. He got you out of jail. There'll surely be a chance to escape.

There wasn't any way she could go back to EGIS. Not if she ever planned to see Sean again. Could she sway Beckett to her side? No. Not likely.

Indigo shut off the water, wrung out her clothing, and hung them on the towel rack. With one hand, she wiped the steam off the mirror, leaving behind a streak. Haunted eyes stared back at her. Once she toweled off, she reached for her wet undergarments and put them on, and then drew on Beckett's shirt. The familiar scent flooded her, niggling at memories best left alone, and she inhaled sharply before lowering the tee from her nose.

A grin flitted across her face. *Of all the gin joints... Casablanca* was one of his favorite movies.

She sobered. This wouldn't be easy. Her body was already betraying her, reminding her how amazing times had been in Beckett's arms. In his bed.

One final glance in the mirror, and she left the room, shorts in hand. Beckett sat in the lone chair between her and the door. While his ball cap hid his gaze, she had no doubt he watched her every move. Had she been fully dressed, she wouldn't be getting by him.

His strong legs stretched out before him; her gaze lingered on the way his jeans molded to them. Dark hair dusted arms she knew to be well muscled. The final remnants of youth had been replaced by a harder edge. Made him more dangerous. More alluring. A bit light-headed at seeing him again, she struggled with the need to touch her throat, as if it could calm the thirst within her.

Had he thought about her? Had he married?

Ignoring the sourness in the pit of her stomach at that thought, she walked to the bed and sat on the edge. His shirt rode high on her thighs. As she expected, a few seconds after she sat, he unfurled his six-three body from the chair and moved toward her.

When they'd first been assigned to partner with one another, she'd wondered how effective a guy his size would be. And his appearance—from that first moment she'd never forgotten his looks. Yet, somehow, people did. He blended with ease, leaving people with the description of a good-looking man, nothing more. Not to mention he had incredible skills, both in and out of the bedroom.

"Talk to me, Indigo. Why were you in a Mexican jail?" His words were controlled, yet she could hear the underlying strain. Seeing her again hadn't been easy on him, either. *Good.* It shouldn't be.

"I attacked some of their men. I 'spect they took exception."

He crouched before her, ripped open an alcohol wipe from the med pack at her side she'd not noticed. The instant his hand landed on her skin, fire shot through her. The coolness of the cloth bit with a painful sting. She welcomed it, because it kept her from focusing on how she'd missed his touch.

"Why would you attack them?"

"They came after me when I went after the men who took Sean."

Blue gaze unerringly met hers. "Fiancé? Boyfriend? Husband?"

She blinked and held his focus. "Son."

Fear lanced her heart at the thought of her precious boy scared and frightened. Swiftly on its heels, however, came anger. White-hot flames burned through her veins. The desire to hunt and kill ran roughshod over her. It took the remaining reserves of her energy to keep motionless. An act that depleted her.

Mentally, she took inventory. Exhausted, hungry, minor injuries—which if untreated could become serious and deadly out here. Yes, Beckett had to take her in, but she could at least get some rest. Perhaps food and a gun. If EGIS had been closer, Beckett would have taken her there instead of stopping here. And she still had time to get where she needed to be.

"Your son? Hey, Indigo." Fingers snapped in front of her face. "Right here. Where's your son?" His thunderous expression shocked her. Why would he care? There wasn't any way he could realize? Right?

"If I knew, he wouldn't be missing." Her words fell sharp and cold.

The tic in his jaw increased as he worked on more of her scrapes. "Who took him?"

"I don't know." She hated the crack in her voice. This was no time to break down. "We were in Puebla to see the Great Pyramid of Cholula. They"—her voice trembled again—"took him right outside our hotel." She gripped his wrist as she spoke. "I tried to get him back. I *tried*."

Beckett moved beside her. "So you fought." He made it a statement, which showed her he took her reaction for granted.

A deep breath. He didn't condemn her; it was understanding and acceptance. "Yes. I took down several of their men before they tased me. I woke up in the cell at the little jail you got me from."

"You're hundreds of miles from Puebla."

She'd been afraid of that. Not willing to let him in on how lost and confused she was, she nodded. "I know." So far, and such a precious item waiting for her to rescue him. Which was why she had to get away.

"And the cops?"

"As far as I can tell, they're in on it. Not in charge, because they only beat me a little."

He went rigid at her statement, his fingers laced with hers—when it had happened she'd no clue—tightening.

"Cops are the ones who bruised your skin?"

She remembered this Beckett. Extremely protective. She glanced at their interlocked fingers. The lingering marks on her and the pain in her ribs were secondary to getting her son back safe and sound.

"Why did you come for me?" She asked the question she'd been wondering since he walked into the jail. Well, not the *only* question.

Indigo knew better than to expect a fairy-tale answer and yet, despite everything, the woman hidden deep inside her wished for one.

"Michael sent me to the jail for an intercept and retrieval. I had no clue it was you until I walked through the door."

Michael. Hearing it was this man worried her, and her mouth went dry. "And he wants you to bring me in."

It wasn't a question. There was no doubt of his orders.

"Yes."

She shook her head. "I won't go."

His chuckle had absolutely no humor in it. "You say that

as if you have a choice."

"There is *always* a choice."

She knew exactly where his thought train went. The concern—and anger on her behalf—disintegrated in a flash. He rose and took two more alcohol wipes, tossing them in her direction.

"Yes, you made that perfectly clear."

There was nothing she could say. Not without getting into feelings she couldn't face now. Her mind took her down roads best left untraveled. To that night—so long ago in humid Louisiana—when she was supposed to meet him. A small, out-of-the-way dive bar where they would blend in easily.

"Nothing to say?"

She made her decision in the space of a heartbeat. "Must be nice to live in your perfect fucking world," she ground out, temper again pricked.

Dark eyebrows slashed down, causing his expression to harden and appear infinitely more dangerous. "What?" He appeared directly before her, making her tip her head back to maintain eye contact. "What did you just say to me?"

"I didn't stutter. You sit there on your high horse, judging me, when you know *nothing* of my life." *He* was the one who hadn't wanted a commitment, marriage, or children, not her. Those words had come from him. Beckett wanted to keep everything light and fun, never getting serious. Then there was that one other issue... She ground her jaw, screaming out her fear and anger on the inside, keeping it all to herself.

His nostrils flared, but he didn't back away. In fact, he came closer, bringing with him the scent of Beckett Hanson—sandalwood, dark amber, and man. Since he hadn't showered yet, she also noticed the salty tang of his sweat. It was *him*. Memories pressed hard. The air rife with tension so thick she could taste it. Their gazes remained locked as they both breathed deep.

"I know."

She swallowed back her tears and focused on her lap, breaking eye contact. Afraid if she didn't, so much more would come tumbling free of her mouth.

Beckett jerked back and stepped away. "Finish cleaning yourself up. We need to get on the road. I'm giving you five minutes, then I'm cuffing you so I can shower."

"Do what you have to." Her voice remained monotone.

She tore open the wipes and did a thorough job of cleaning out the remaining cuts, then pulled on her damp shorts, opting to continue wearing his shirt. A throbbing began in the back of her head, and she willed it away. Matching wits with a man who knew her extremely well would be difficult enough without having a headache.

True to his word, exactly five minutes later, he cuffed her to the headboard. And not in a way she could escape, either. She bit back the moan of pain when he put up her left arm; the landing from the moving truck had done more than she'd first anticipated.

Heat flared in his gaze as it roved over her secured body. He cuffed her hands to the headboard as she sat against it; he used rope to bind her legs to the corner posts on the footboard. Refusing to allow her body to betray her more, she closed her eyes, shutting him out.

"Why don't you just ask me?"

His statement had her looking at him again. Crap. She'd not been expecting what waited for her. Beckett stood there, shirtless, and all too tempting. Moisture gathered in her mouth while her fingers tingled with the need to touch him. Bronzed skin with a few scars here and there. It just wasn't fair. The man was gorgeous. No bones about it. And she knew every inch of his hard body. In another time and place, they would be exploring each other and nothing else would matter but the passion between them. The cuffs preventing her from running would be used for a different reason. One of pleasure and fun.

"What is it exactly you believe I should just ask you?"

He barely blinked. "To help you."

She narrowed her eyes at him. Well, he'd brought it up, so she might as well go with it. Sitting up higher with as much dignity she could manage, she took a deep breath, licked her lips, and sighed. "Help me get Sean back. Don't take me to EGIS, where you know damn well I'll not be allowed to leave." Not in time to do what she had to, to save her son.

"You disappeared. What the hell was that all about?"

She swallowed. He didn't know about that night in Louisiana. About Sean. "You wanted me to ask you to help me. That's what I'm doing. I'm not answering questions about that night." A brief pause. "Or anything else."

"You want my help, Iggy, you have to give me the answers I want. I have no problem taking you in."

Iggy. His pet name and endearment for her. How many nights had she longed to hear it just one more time? His saying it now, after all these years, set off a kaleidoscope of butterflies in her gut, all of them winging up at once. But the resulting tremor wasn't anything she was ready to face. "I know you'd have no problem turning me over to EGIS, even if I *do* answer your questions."

"True. However, I'm the one in the position to ask the questions. So, tell me why I should help you."

A myriad of explanations floated around in her mind, reasons to secure the assistance of this man in recovering her son. But that would be playing mind games, and frankly, she had neither the energy nor the time to waste.

"I could give you a whole bunch of bullshit answers to sway you to my side. I won't say anything but this. If you'll only help me for one reason—or hell, not even me, but Sean—then it's this. Sole reason." She took a deep breath before admitting the secret she'd carried for nearly eight years. Never telling him because he hadn't wanted a long-term commitment, and he worked for the company she'd run from. It wasn't a good mix. Not any of it.

"Sean is yours."

Chapter Two

Shit.

"What did you say?" Beckett stepped toward her, then stopped. If he hadn't been hearing things, he might put his hands on her. To shake her. Hard.

She swallowed yet never dropped her gaze. In fact, she barely moved except rotating her wrists in the cuffs. "I said Sean is your son."

His knees threatened to buckle. Shoring himself, he shook his head. Lies. He crossed his arms and glowered at her. "Don't you think that's an excessive stretch to get my help? That's a low blow even for *you*, Indigo."

He watched her face, expecting to see shame or a small bit of embarrassment. Nothing.

"You *are* his father, Beckett."

"How old is he?"

She gave him a bland stare. "Are you going to help me?"

"And if I say no?"

Not even a shrug. "That's your decision, and we're back to where we started. You doing what you think you should, and me doing what I *have* to."

Have to. "How old is he?" A slow, burning anger began to boil in his stomach.

"Seven." She shifted, the handcuffs rubbing along the wood. "He was conceived in Africa. Sudan."

"Tell me you're lying." He heard the begging in his tone. A son? He had a son? He clenched his fists. "Tell me you didn't keep a child from me." Was that his voice sounding all strained? Yes.

He strove to remain calm, but he truly wanted to yell and demand. Shake her and figure out what the hell she meant. Was it the truth? The look on her face was one of resignation. She wouldn't have told him if she didn't think he'd change his mind and help her. That cut him deep.

Why would she have kept that from him? Surely it wasn't because all those years ago he'd allowed some of the dumbest words ever to slide free of his mouth about not wanting kids.

Whirling around, he went to shower, his anger so massive he shook from the force of it. He kept it quick, because he wouldn't put another escape attempt past her. The cuffs wouldn't hold her forever. Indigo was far too smart to not figure out a way to escape.

Dried and dressed, he pushed back into the room and opened his mouth to say something, only to pause. Her eyes had closed, head drooped forward, the cuffs on her wrists the only things holding her up. He walked closer on silent feet, alert for a fast movement or attack. No movement from her. Indigo had fallen asleep. He settled along her left side and blew out a breath. Exhaustion lined her face. Dark circles beneath her eyes and a bruise on her left cheek. Right now, however, she appeared almost peaceful, and his heart—traitorous thing it was—skipped a few beats as he sat beside her.

"Damn you, Iggy." He untied her ankles. Had things been different, they both would have enjoyed her being tied up as she was. But they weren't.

His curse was soft, so it didn't wake her. He reached out a hand and tucked some hair behind her ear. He had no choice. Not now. Were he honest and truthful with himself, he'd acknowledge his choice had died the second he knew his retrieval was her. He wondered if Michael knew and had sent him for the intercept for this very reason.

After grabbing his key, he undid her cuffs, readjusting to lay her flat on the bed before covering her with a blanket. She barely stirred, and he knew just how wiped she must be. Right here, she was the woman he remembered loving so fully, completely, and without any reserve. Thick lashes rested against her cheeks, full lips slightly parted as she breathed deeply.

Was he pleased with her revelation? No. Not a way to find out he had a son. How much he'd missed. Her pregnancy. First step. First word. He exhaled with frustration.

Moving away, he grabbed his phone and dialed a number. It was answered swiftly.

"Where are you?"

"A hotel room."

He sat back on the bed, resting against the headboard. Reaching over, he tugged up the blanket on Indigo, then crossed his ankles.

"I told you to get back here. Not stop for a fuck."

When Michael wasn't happy, his dirty mouth tended to get worse. Beckett shook his head but hesitated from speaking for, at that moment, Indigo rolled up against him. He closed his eyes as she burrowed tight to him, the way she used to sleep before. All up on him, as if she couldn't get close enough.

"We didn't stop for a fuck, as you so eloquently put it. You told me to get off the road. It's hot as crap out there, and she was bleeding. I didn't think I should pull into a gas station with a woman dripping blood all over the passenger seat."

"I don't care of you have to knock her out, put her in the back of the truck, and cover her with a tarp to get her here, just do it."

"What justification could EGIS have for bringing her in?" Or was it Michael who wanted her? And why did that make his protective instincts rush to the surface?

No matter what, the man had his loyalty. Michael had rescued him from ten years of living on the streets, steered him in the right direction, and given him purpose, as well as helping him reunite with his birth sister. He'd been hard, but he'd never given up on Beckett. Working for EGIS was his life and something he loved doing more than anything. He focused on the woman beside him. Almost anything.

"I told you, Beckett. I'll let you in on it when she gets here. Not before." Michael was angry.

He's hiding something. It wasn't uncommon for Michael to keep things to himself. Normally, Beckett didn't mind and would follow orders. This was different. It involved Iggy, and he was all about protecting this woman. She'd been his partner for years and deserved the benefit of the doubt, regardless of how she'd left him. If his choice meant going against Michael and EGIS? He wasn't sure he was ready to face the answer for that yet. "We have to get going."

"Good. See you soon."

He ended the call and set his phone beside his thigh. Dropping his head back, he groaned. Things had just gotten all kinds of complicated.

With a quick check of his watch, he slipped reluctantly from the bed and the woman who'd curled up to him. He could give her a few more minutes of sleep.

It didn't take him long to pack up; she slumbered, so he carried her to the truck. The fact she didn't stir told him she'd succumbed to her stress and exhaustion. Her small measure of trust was telling. And humbling. And how amazing she felt in his arms. He drove through a small town where he got gas, a map, and some prepackaged sandwiches and chips, then got them on their way.

Indigo woke an hour later. She didn't move, but he knew she'd come alert. He had the second she woke.

"There's food in the bags by your feet. And water. You need to drink some so you don't dehydrate more than you are."

She didn't speak, and he bit back a frustrated growl.

"Don't think about jumping, Iggy. We're going about seventy, and despite my orders, we're on our way to Puebla. So keep your ass glued in the goddamn seat."

"Puebla?" The small bit of hope in her voice was like a defibrillator on his heart. Oh, man, he was so fucked. How he was going to survive without losing his heart all over again, he hadn't the slightest clue. That, of course, assumed he hadn't lost it already.

The warm feeling faded when he remembered how she'd denied him the simple opportunity to know his own child, be part of his life. Not to mention why she'd just disappeared without a word. That was upsetting enough, but paled in comparison to the fact she'd kept his son from him.

That would help him survive this: the anger.

"Yes. And since it's going to be a long drive, you can tell me why the *fuck* you kept my son from me, and why you didn't *call* me the second he vanished." He took a deep breath. "Then we'll move on to what happened that night in Louisiana when you stood me up at that bar and I never saw you again until today. Why I'm pulled off an op and sent to some hellhole where the first thing that greets me when I walk in the door is the dulcet tones of you threatening to cut off a guy's dick and feed it to him in pieces."

He heard her riffling through the bags at her feet, which was followed by her opening a bottle of water. "I was out. Out of the game. I made the decision to quit the moment I learned I was pregnant. I almost told Michael but changed my mind and made the decision to go off the grid. It didn't matter. I'm positive he knew before *I* did. He always seemed to know more than he should. Maybe he discovered I was pregnant, too. I wasn't going to bring my child into that life. I couldn't. The only way to get out completely was to go dark."

Beckett respected that decision, because he wouldn't want to raise a child while living the life of an operative. The subterfuge. The lies. The risk. However, he *was* the father, according to her. Therefore, her choice sucked because it kept him in the dark, too. "You didn't tell me. Why?"

He could feel the shrug she gave. "No real reason. I'm pragmatic and decided to deal with it on my own. I didn't want to fight with you about it. I wasn't going to have an abortion, and you'd told me you didn't want children. I'm not telling you this because I want you in his life. If I could do this without you, I wouldn't have said anything at all."

Her answer was brutally honest, and he flexed his fingers on the wheel. He'd figured those words would come back to haunt him. It had been a stupid fight they had about a future, and he'd said he didn't want children. Iggy did. Hearing her response, without a shred of emotion in her voice, tore at him.

"So you really thought I wouldn't help you find *our* son?" God, did she view him as such a bastard? Son. He had a son. It wasn't digesting well and seemed almost like a fog had surrounded him. He shook his head to clear it.

A son. He was a father. *Christ.*

She didn't speak for a few minutes, and he was about to ask her again when she said, "I was there, you know. I came."

He frowned and swerved to avoid a nocturnal animal slowly crossing the road. "There, where?"

"Snakes."

Snakes. The dive bar where they were supposed to meet. He glanced in her direction, barely making out her features in the faded glow from the dashboard lights.

"You were there?" He'd waited an hour and never saw her.

"I was. But so was Michael. I wasn't about to risk your career as well as our…relationship by making myself known."

"I would have known if you'd been there." Wouldn't he? Bigger question, why had Michael been there? What had he been after?

"For what it's worth, I'm sorry."

Sorry. She was sorry she'd vanished without a word. He ground his jaw and breathed deep. "Has Michael been looking for you all this time?"

"I don't know. Maybe. I don't understand why. Surely by now he's gotten over my leaving. I left him short an agent, but it happens. He has no reason to be after me."

"What else do you know about the ones who took Sean?"

A ragged sigh filled the cab, followed by the sounds of her drinking. "Nothing. They spoke Spanish, mostly talking crap. They could have been hired goons. I don't know what or who they are. I'm not a threat to anyone anymore. I'm a mother trying to make the best life she can for her son."

Oh, she was a threat, all right, a serious one to him, but he didn't need to tell her that, either. "Were you given any instructions?"

"Yes."

"And?" he prompted when she didn't continue.

"I have to get to a mailbox by a certain time or they'll kill Sean."

And cops were holding her, so she couldn't get there. It didn't make sense. "When?" Fear clenched at his heart and lungs, making it hard to breathe.

"Tomorrow afternoon."

"What?"

"This is why I've been trying so hard to get away. I'm sorry about running before, but I'll do anything to get there and keep my son safe."

He pressed on the accelerator, and they sped away into the night. He'd be damned if he lost the opportunity to spend time with his son before he'd even met him.

• • •

She glowered at the idiot standing before her. "What do you mean, Indigo Grey's not in jail? Isn't that what I paid you for? To take her there and kill her? We finally locate her, set it up so she's arrested and kept in one place until we can get her, and you're telling me she's not there?" The only other sound in the room was that of her nails as she drummed them on the smooth teak top of her desk. Her tone had less warmth in it than a polar ice cap as she glared at the man doing his damnedest not to fidget while he stood in front of her desk.

"The man who picked her up wasn't the one we sent."

She closed her eyes and struggled to contain her anger. She despised incompetence. "What happened to your man?"

He cleared his throat as a bead of sweat ran along his receding hairline. "Detained."

She gazed about her office, nearly submerged in darkness. Pinching the bridge of her nose, she crossed one leg over the other, noting how her hose made her legs so smooth. "By whom?" She had a good idea on who was behind this, however: EGIS.

"He didn't give his name, Madam. The officers say he was tall, wore a ball cap, and, well, looked like anyone who'd come there. We picked the small station so there wouldn't be lots of questions and the personnel could be bribed."

She clenched her jaw. "I'm well aware of why the area was picked." She typed on her keyboard, the sound ominous in the gloom. "My question is, why do I pay you if I end up having to take care of this anyway?" She tapped the enter key with more force than necessary. "I took care of it. They won't make it back to Puebla."

"What about the child?"

She scowled. "I don't give a damn what he does with the brat. Sell him, kill him, makes no difference to me. He can do whatever he wants. Nothing, however, I repeat *nothing* is to be done to the kid until I get verification she's been killed."

The man lingered for a moment longer until she lifted an eyebrow at him. He gulped and left, pivoting on his heels; in moments, she was alone in her office.

She made some notes in an encrypted file, explaining how things would have to be altered. A minor bump, but the men she had on the job now would be successful. Indigo Grey would be dead soon, and her problems would be over.

After closing the lid on her computer, she rose from her chair and walked to the small door that opened when she turned a statue on a shelf. She stepped through and moved closer to the large bed and the man lying naked on it. He was younger than her, but she didn't care. He was what she wanted. At least when the one who she'd do anything for wasn't around.

"Problems?" he asked, stroking himself as he watched her undress.

"Minor."

He narrowed his gaze. "I dislike problems."

She hitched up her skirt as she crawled on the bed, joining him. Once she reached him, she straddled him and sank on his erect length, grateful for her crotchless pantyhose and lack of a thong.

"It's not a problem. I took care of it. She'll be dead, he can do what he wants with the brat, and then we can have him killed, too."

He gripped her hips, halting her motion. "Who got her?"

"EGIS."

"How did they find out she was down there?"

"I don't know. I do know Beckett was sent to get her." The lie slid from her lips like a hockey player across the ice, smooth and easy. There were times it paid to play both sides. Lying was a necessity in her line of work, just like sleeping with whomever to get what she wanted.

"Do you think DeSalvo told EGIS?"

"I doubt it." She pursed her lips. "I think even *he* knows better than to cross us. I'll trace the leak later. Right now, I have things I want more." She dug her nails into his chest, loving the way he gasped as she drew blood. The flash in his eyes warned her of retaliation. She gave him a catlike grin. She wanted it all.

. . .

Indigo rolled her shoulders as she kept her gaze on the horizon. The wheel beneath her fingers jumped occasionally as she kept the truck on the road. Beside her, Beckett slept. In her peripheral vision, she stared at the man who'd stolen her heart years ago and had given her the most precious item in the world: Sean.

The morning sun cast a golden glow over Beckett, reminding her how things had been between them at one time. He'd never treated her any differently when they were around the others. However, when they were just the two of them, he was attentive, loving, and protective. Not that he ever doubted she could do her job—he was just defensive in the way of a man keeping his woman safe. And that's what she was, his woman. Not was. Had been.

He'd taken the news of Sean very well. That bothered her. It had gone smoothly, almost too smoothly. The Beckett she remembered had been a bit hotheaded, but this one, he seemed almost too contained. She let it go, accepting they'd both changed over the years.

Part of her rebelled against not trusting him fully but this was about Sean, and until her son was back in her arms, everyone was suspect. Although, of all the people she could possibly have at her side, Beckett would be the man she'd pick.

In the rearview mirror, she noticed another vehicle speeding along. She tensed and wished for a better truck.

"Beckett," she said.

"Hmm?" He stirred and looked at her from beneath the brim of his hat, those gorgeous eyes of his sleepy and sexy.

"We've got company coming up fast on our six. Black SUV."

He sat up, all traces of sleep wiped clean. Glancing over his shoulder, he frowned and reached down for his sidearm.

"What do you think?" she asked, watching the narrow road ahead of her, along with keeping an eye on the approaching Suburban.

"Government issue. Keep going, and we'll see."

She swallowed and did as he said. Her breaths came a bit easier when he slipped a weapon under her thigh. The car behind her shifted to the other lane, and she saw another racing behind it.

Beckett's muttered curse told her he'd noticed, too. When the first shot came, she was ready, already turning the wheel, instinct taking over. Bullets sprayed across the back window, and they both ducked.

"Shit! Hang on."

She gunned the engine and asked for everything the truck could give. Unfortunately, it wasn't as much juice as their attackers could get from their newer, more powerful vehicles. They were outmatched. Regardless, she wasn't going without a fight.

The windows were already down because of the lack of air-conditioning, and she gave a nod in response to Beckett's silent question. He fired at the windshield and then kicked it out. She squinted against pieces of glass, which sprayed past her.

"Ready?" he hollered over the wind that poured into the cab.

No. Christ, this wasn't her life anymore. "As I'll ever be."

With a deep breath, she spun the truck so it raced backward. Beckett took out the vehicle on the other side of the road while she fired at the one that had been behind them. It swerved, lost control, and went off the blacktop, then rolled over a few times to a stop.

She slowed down, changed gears, drove closer, and shut off the engine. Glock in hand, she got out, Beckett mimicking on the other side. They moved first to the SUV he'd taken out. Two men lying across the seats, stunned. He pulled them out, tied them up, and stripped them of all weapons. Then they went to the other vehicle. Those two were dead. She could care less.

They took the weapons from them, too, and headed back to the first SUV, which was still usable. While Beckett questioned them, she changed the flat tire with the spare and got the vehicle back on the heated road surface. The day, while early, already had her sweating. Transferring all their things from the small truck to the SUV, she waited for him.

"What do you want to do with them?"

"Shoot them." She barely looked at the men. "I doubt they'll talk, and I don't have time for them to change their minds.

"You want to kill them?" The surprise in his voice should have shocked her.

"They would have done the same to us without hesitation. Do it or don't. I don't care. They may or may not survive out here in the heat with no water." She shrugged and put four shots into the truck's engine block. "I don't think they're going anywhere unless they walk."

She had no remorse. They'd fucked with her son, tried to kill her, and she'd kill every last one of them she had to in order to get him back. After opening the driver's door, she hopped in and started it up. The air blew through, and she smiled at the immediate relief. Then she frowned. She'd worked hard to lose that cold edge working with EGIS had given her. Sean had changed her, allowing her to be someone who cared about others. Until the moment they took her son from her. All of that fell away.

Moments later, Beckett joined her. She got them back on their way as he dug through the glove box to try to see if the men had left anything behind that could be useful.

"Did they say anything?"

"Nothing useful," he replied, slamming the glove box door shut and settling back with a groan. "Kept saying how they didn't know anything about a boy. They were after you."

"That's what I thought," she muttered, dread filling her.

"What I don't understand is why is all this happening now? I've been off the grid for eight years. Why bring me out here to kill me? Why not just gun me down by the hotel? Drive-bys happen all the time. I'm missing something."

She didn't include Beckett in her ramblings; she had to figure this EGIS problem out herself. And she would. The one thing she'd never question was his loyalty to EGIS. It ran deep. He lived and breathed for them. When she'd been active with them, her dedication had been close to his but not as serious. She'd loved her job, but everything had changed when Sean began growing in her.

Michael would have used her son to get her to do things. He had no qualms about using people, although she didn't hold that against him. But she had no intentions of allowing him to do that with her baby.

So what intel did she have?

She was exhausted, beat, and sore. She had a kidnapped son and was working tentatively beside his father, who happened to be a steadfast EGIS agent. People were out to kill her—nothing new, but it had been a while. So why kidnap Sean? Dread nearly overwhelmed her. The ideas forming didn't sketch the prettiest of pictures.

She pushed the vehicle hard. They stopped for gas and a restroom break, but she was getting nervous. Her time limit fast approached, and she wasn't at the drop box yet. Not nearly close enough.

"We'll make it," Beckett assured her as they hurried back to the SUV. "You take a nap, I'll drive." His tone brooked no room for disagreement and for a minute, she was reminded of how he could comfort her with nothing more than a few words. His confidence that it would work out, supreme and unchallengeable.

She didn't want to, but she wasn't so stupid as to think she didn't need rest. Without argument, she climbed in the passenger side, drank some water, and reclined in the seat.

He woke her as they entered Puebla. Feeling better, she sat up and gave him directions to the mailbox.

"Drop me off about a block or two away. I don't want them thinking I came with help if they're watching the area."

"No way. I'm not letting you do this alone."

She reined in her anger. "This is the only way I can find out what I have to do to get Sean back."

"Not happening." He veered off and pulled up behind a small taxi. "Let's go."

She understood what he intended and hopped out. Soon, he'd rented the cab, having given the older gentleman more money than he'd have made all day. Sliding in the backseat, she met Beckett's cobalt gaze in the mirror. No words spoken, but she knew he understood her thanks.

Beckett pulled up in front of the mail place and idled the car. Indigo climbed out and headed in without a look back; he'd stay and keep an eye out for her. After making her way to the narrow counter, she waited for someone to acknowledge her. Two other men pretended interest in their mailboxes. She knew better. Both men were packing and were there to watch her.

"*Sí?*" A slender, dark-haired woman approached.

"I'm here to pick up something for Isabella Grant." That was the name they'd told her it would be under.

The woman smiled at her, all bubbly and infectious. "Right. I have it right here. One moment." She slipped into the back and returned carrying a manila envelope. "Here you go."

"Thank you." Without wasting time, Indigo hurried back out to the waiting taxi and climbed in.

"Well?"

"Drive. Let's go."

So he did. She opened the envelope and pulled out a throwaway phone and some folded papers. A picture of her son slid out, and she gasped when she saw the paper beside him, the knot in her belly subsiding slightly. That was today's date. *Thank you, Jesus.*

"What's wrong?"

"Nothing yet. They just added a picture of Sean." Her mind whirled, and she needed to take a minute. Her son was *okay*. For the moment, but he was okay. Her hand trembled as she set the picture aside.

Opening the rest of the sheets, she frowned at the images. "If you're sure no one is following, can you get us back to the SUV or to a hotel?"

"I want to see that picture when we get there."

Of course he did. Not that she blamed him—she'd dropped the bomb on him about the boy he'd never met.

Soon they were back in the SUV, driving through the city looking for a place to stay. She couldn't return to the room she and Sean had shared. If the kidnappers were good, and by all accounts they were, that room would have been vacated and her things gone. The phone from the envelope lit up and rang. No number came on the screen, it merely said, "Blocked."

She shared a look with Beckett in the rearview, then put it to her ear. "Hello?"

"Did you see the pictures?" A man's voice, with a slight

Hispanic accent.

"Yes. Who is this?"

"I ask questions, bitch. Not you."

She ground her teeth to control her temper.

"You will kill these men."

"All of them?" She blinked and stared at the images on her lap. Ten men. Seriously?

"Yes. You have ten days."

"Let me talk to my son."

"You see picture, today's date."

"That's the first edition of the paper. I want to speak to him to know you haven't done anything to him." Her gut churned with nausea.

Spanish curses filled her ears, but soon a child's voice piped up. "Mama?"

Oh, sweet Jesus. Tears ran down her cheeks at the sound of his voice. "Sean? Are you okay, baby?" Her hand shook so bad she almost dropped the phone.

"Are you coming to get me soon, Mama? I want to go home. I don't want to stay here anymore."

Her chest hurt. "I'm on my way, baby. I'll be there just as soon as I can." She worked hard to keep the tears and her fear from her voice. He needed to be brave and strong. A feat that would be more difficult if his mother was a wailing mess.

"Okay." She heard the quaver in his voice and craved to hold him.

"I love you," she said.

"How sweet," said the adult male voice, laden with sarcasm. "You want to see boy again, you do as we say."

She was going to kill him for touching her son. "How am

I supposed to do this?"

"Not my problem. You figure it out."

"Ten is a lot to kill. I need weapons and money. I wasn't exactly packed for this kind of thing when I came here on *vacation*. Next to that, there was being tasered and beaten by what I assume to be your boys."

Behind the wheel, Beckett stiffened and stared at her once more, his gaze locking with hers in the rectangular mirror.

She heard a muffled argument. Perhaps they didn't know she'd been tasered and beaten.

"You need, I get. But no tricks."

"Buddy, you've got my son. I'm not playing with his life. I'll want to talk to him twice a day so I know he's okay. Morning and night."

"No."

"Fine, then every other day."

"Maybe. I'm in control. Not you."

She clenched her fist and strove with everything inside her for restraint. "I have to look over this, and I'll call you back with a list of what I'm going to need."

The pause had her wondering if he truly were in charge. "Two hours. I call you."

He was gone after giving her the number.

Chapter Three

Beckett swore, something he'd been doing a lot more of since Indigo Grey had been shoved back into his life. She was in her hotel room right now. He had a key; she'd covertly slipped one in his pocket as she moved by him in a crowd, but he had to give it a bit before he went to her room. Normally he understood the waiting game. But time was short, and he really wanted to be there with her.

Shouldering his bag, he rambled to the stairs and up. This place didn't have an elevator. It was small and off the main drag in the city, so they wouldn't attract attention.

He slipped into her room and saw her standing off to the left side, Glock drawn and aimed unerringly at his head. She didn't lower it until he'd entered fully and closed the door behind him, proving he hadn't been followed. He could tell she had no wish to put it down. She still didn't trust him.

He didn't get what her problem was. He wasn't the one who'd lied about a child all these years. Yep, the bitterness lingered. And it would for a while, but right now he had to stay focused and help save this son of his before he never got to meet him.

Indigo didn't speak, just went back to the papers spread over the narrow bed and sat. The pistol rested right by her thigh, where her fingers occasionally touched it, as if she needed the reassurance. A familiar weapon helped center her.

"What'd you figure out?" he asked. She wouldn't volunteer information to him. This woman was not the same one he'd partnered with in the past. That Indigo had never been a chatterbox, but she understood his thoughts, shared intel, and they'd worked together like a well-oiled machine.

"I don't see how I can avoid killing these people."

Just when he thought he had her figured out, she went and changed on him. He could hear the distress in her tone. In the past, it was just a job; she'd never hesitated to fulfill a kill order.

"I don't trust them not to change it. They want me to fail."

"I'm calling in EGIS."

As his words faded from the air, he saw her weapon leveled at his head. Her stare eerily blank and dead. "Don't do anything that would make me have to kill you."

Cold. Brutally honest. Her gaze like ice as she watched him, waiting for him to make his move. No doubt she'd pull the trigger.

He held up his hands to keep them from where his own firearm rested. "Hear me out, Indigo. They can help. This is massive. Too big for only us to do alone in the allotted time."

"Michael gets his hands on me, and I can kiss my son's life good-bye. He wants me for something, and I'd be at his mercy until he got whatever it was. He'll lock me up. We both know it." Her hand wavered, and Beckett took a step closer. Her weapon steadied in a heartbeat, and he drew up.

She had a point. But… "You've been out for eight years. I have no idea why he'd want to lock you up. I won't let him touch you."

She didn't so much as blink. Okay, now that hurt. Why didn't she trust him? He blew out a breath and moved forward. She tracked him with her eyes, but when her finger slipped from the side of the barrel to curl around the trigger, he swallowed hard. He decided to trust his gut. It told him she didn't *want* to shoot him. But would she?

"You want to shoot me, Iggy, go ahead. But I'm not stopping."

He finished closing the distance between them, all the while hoping she wouldn't actually shoot him. Her hand shook by the time he reached her, and he plucked the pistol from her grip. He tossed it on the bed to be lost among the photos.

She looked up at him, and he just couldn't help himself. Cupping her face in his hands, fingers delving in her hair, he stroked his thumbs along her lower lip. Nose to nose, he closed his eyes and kissed her. Keeping it gentle, he dragged his tongue along the seam of her lips, asking for permission. When she opened beneath his touch, he sank into the heat of her mouth.

Iggy. His Iggy. She responded with a moan, arching closer into him, wrapping her arms around him, breasts tight to his chest. Lowering her until her back pressed against the mattress, he deepened the kiss. Lust slammed into him. So long—it had been so long since this woman had been in his arms. A blessing or a curse, perhaps that was a blessing *and* a curse.

Breaking the kiss, he rose up and stared at her. Every part of him wanted to continue down the road where nothing mattered but the two of them and the passion between them. "Trust me, Iggy. Sean is my son, too." He narrowed his gaze. "Despite you not wanting me to know about him." The words were harsh and sharp.

Resignation and uncertainty filled her gaze. "Call them in, then. When Michael locks me up, I'll escape. And when I do, it would be in your best interest not to come after me, because I'll kill you. Nothing and no one will stand between me and my son."

She spoke the truth. Just one correction. "Our son, Iggy. *Our* son. And had you trusted me earlier, we might not be in this situation."

Backing up, he pulled his phone free and stared at the numbers, ignoring the pain his words put in her gaze, weighing the options of calling in EGIS.

Before he could dial, a knock came to the door. He immediately went for his sidearm. Beckett frowned and faced the door. He wasn't surprised when Iggy stood at an angle from him, her piece aimed at the opening.

He paced slowly to the door and opened it, trusting her to shoot if it was necessary. Michael stood there, a scowl on his tanned face.

"Holed up in a fucking hotel room," he snapped. "Take her."

"No!" he cried as two men brushed by him. Beckett launched a punch, taking one out. Three shots echoed, and his world went black.

· · ·

Beckett stirred and sat slowly. The darkness surrounding him took a few moments to adjust to. He blinked and frowned as the interior of the plane came into focus.

Fucking shit. "Tell me you didn't do what I think you did," he groused.

"Then don't ask." Michael's tone, uninterested and cold, came from his left.

He angled his head and found his boss sitting there, illuminated by the track lightning on the floor. Michael's blond hair was a bit shaggy, the ends touching a blue-and-white floral shirt, his blue eyes shuttered, his expression bland. He had the physique of a linebacker who played the occasional pickup game and stayed in shape.

"Why?" Beckett rubbed his head, unable to get rid of the ache.

"I wanted her back at EGIS, not with you elsewhere in Mexico." He sipped his drink, his shadow as elusive and shifty as the man himself.

"You don't know what you've done," he said, panic increasing in time with his anger. "Where is she?"

The plane's interior lights flickered on, and Michael gestured behind him. Beckett rose, wishing the cloudiness would leave, and stumbled back to find her.

Indigo sat in the very last row, one man beside her and another across from her, his back to Beckett. She wore a four-piece restraint and was as tranquil as death, despite the band around her waist connecting the cuffs on her hands and the ones on her ankles to the chair.

"Is she sleeping?" he demanded.

One man shrugged. "No clue. She hasn't said a word."

"Move," he barked to the man facing her. The moment he vacated that seat, Beckett took it. The second he sat, her eyes popped open, homing in on him like a cruise missile. Had there been anger or rage burning in her gaze he would have understood. Any type of emotion, hatred or something. But there was nothing. She just stared at him.

Beckett didn't much care for the warning signals his body gave him. The words she'd uttered to him before EGIS had shown up rang loud and clear in his mind. She meant them.

"Leave," he said to the other man, who sat nearby. Soon Beckett sat alone with her. "I'm sorry, Indigo."

She blinked, then turned her attention out the window to stare at something only she saw.

"I swear I had no idea he'd pull something like this." Nothing from her. "Damn it! Would you say something?" Guilt gnawed at his gut. This was his fault. He'd been so focused on her, he'd forgotten about the tracker in his phone. This was his doing, their being captured.

She turned her head so their gazes met. Again, it was for the barest fraction of time before she glanced away, cutting him off as succinctly as slamming a door in his face.

"I'll fix this, Iggy. I *swear* I will." He rose and walked back to where Michael sat, drink in hand. "You need to let her go."

"Not a chance, Hanson. And you're not helping her orchestrate any escape attempts, either."

"You're putting her child in danger."

"I doubt it. Women have been lying for years, Beckett.

It's a fact of life."

"I believe her. You didn't see her expression."

He waved a hand. "Save your spiel, it's not happening."

Beckett returned to his seat, anger coursing through him with every pump of his heart. He didn't understand why Michael was acting this way. At all.

What could he do while they were up here? Nothing. He didn't fly, so he couldn't take over the plane. But he could help her once they landed.

Indigo never spoke. Not for the rest of the flight, the ride in the SUV, or when she was put in an interrogation room.

He was ordered away from her, and after a trip to his room, he strode toward Michael's office.

"Hi, Julie," he said to Michael's secretary, halting her conversation on the phone. "I need to speak to him."

She gave him a brief smile. "Sorry, Mr. Hanson. Mr. Wythe isn't available."

"If he's in there, he's available."

"He went to question Indigo." She picked up a pencil. "Is there a message I can deliver to him?"

"No, I'll find him down there. Thank you." Beckett marched to the room where Indigo was being held. He stepped into the observation area and watched through the one-way glass. She sat in the room, alone. Michael hadn't arrived yet. She didn't move, didn't fidget. Just sat and waited.

The door banged open, and she moved so little he wondered if she breathed.

"Welcome home, Indigo," Michael said.

• • •

The chair beneath her was hard and uncomfortable, yet Indigo sat immobile, eyes downcast as she waited for what was to come. Michael bursting through the door hadn't surprised her in the least. The same four-piece he'd slapped her in on the plane still restrained her. As if she were some lifer in a maximum-security prison.

She could be dangerous but preferred not to be. However, this was the best way for him to be safe, because if her hands were free she'd kill him.

Another guard followed Michael in and closed them in together.

"No comment?" Michael asked. "Look at me."

The man wore a hideous floral shirt and baggy white shorts with sandals. Typical Michael Wythe.

"Been a while." He crossed his arms and leaned against the door, blocking her only exit, unless she went through the third-story window or took him out. An option, not really viable or desirable, but…doable if necessary.

She nearly hissed in anger. "You want to share a hug? Sing a folk song?"

"Still a bitch."

She barely blinked. "I'm sorry. Was I supposed to change for you? You still wear your repugnant flower shirts and act like the world is your play toy."

He scowled and waved off her comment. "A son?" He lifted his brows. "You never said you were pregnant. Who's the father?"

"At which point in my life did I say you have the right be in my business?"

He glared. "When you came to work for EGIS."

Definitely not how she recalled it. "Which I no longer

do. So let's both cut the shit. What am I doing here?"

Tension in the room shot up. She didn't buy his relaxed position for an instant. Michael was a crafty bastard. *Let me go, you jackass.* He was putting her son's life in danger.

"I thought you were seeing Beckett."

She waited for him to continue.

"The two of you were screwing each another on missions. I even followed him one night to Snakes. Thought he was meeting you. Never saw you, but I did see the blonde twins he left with that night."

Maintaining her bland expression, she stifled a yawn. "Is this where I'm supposed to be asking you about the women he left with? If you're trying to get a rise out of me, you're going to have to do much better than that. I'm a mother who's focused on one thing only. Saving her son's life." Only with incredible strength did she keep her desperation from her tone.

"Where're the money and weapons you took?"

She frowned and struggled not to lean back in shock at his question. "Excuse me? What money and weapons?"

"The ones you stole from EGIS."

What the fuck was he talking about? She hadn't expected that. "Is that why you wanted Beckett to intercept me? In hopes I'd reveal some location to you? I don't know what you're talking about. How did you find out I was in jail?"

He waved his hand, dismissing her question. Michael approached the table and placed his hands on the top.

"You left, it was gone. Where's my stuff?"

Despite how the man dressed, he could be extremely intimidating when he wanted to be. Bottom line, she'd have to be insane to steal from EGIS. But that was a concern for another time. Right now, she needed to get out of here and find a way back to Mexico to save Sean.

"You're not going to believe me no matter what I say, so it's pointless to continue this discussion. I'm shocked you had to call in extra security. For what? Me? I'm a mother who bakes cookies and is a member of the PTA. How much of a threat can I be to the head of EGIS?" His gaze narrowed. She shifted her weight on the chair, the chains binding her not making a sound. "Or do you think I have a weapon somewhere on me that was missed when I was searched, and I'll shoot you dead, not going for a mere flesh wound?" The guard straightened and focused on her, a soullessness she recognized. The man would blindly follow any order, and right now he'd been ordered to protect Michael against anything. Including her.

"You talk too much, Indigo."

"You wanted me talking just a few moments ago. What, now I should stop?" She canted her head to the side. "Let's keep this going. Why don't we tell everyone how you left one of your team to die because you didn't want any blowback if it went wrong?"

Anger flashed in his eyes, and the fist on the table clenched before he shook his head. "Enough."

"I don't know, there're a lot of things I could say, and if you're planning on locking me up and throwing away the key, what's to keep me from talking now, where all these people can hear the recording?"

"Get out," he barked at the guard.

The man left, unable to hide the curiosity on his face. Michael faced her again.

"What do you want?"

"I want my son, and I want to get out of here." She leaned forward. "More than that, I *never* want to see your face again."

"Give me my money and weapons, and you can leave."

"Bullshit. Even if I *had* taken whatever you think I did, the moment I gave it to you I'd be locked up for theft. We both know I never took anything. You want your pound of flesh for me leaving you high and dry. Then again, maybe you have an entirely different reason for wanting me here." She shook her head and readjusted on the seat. "I told you when I first signed on with EGIS you wouldn't be able to control me, and if I felt as if I were being manipulated or used I'd leave. Do you remember that conversation?"

"We caught the guy," he said, sounding like a petulant child.

"I don't care. You used me. Without my knowledge. All you had to do was ask, and I would have helped."

"You and Beckett were getting too close."

You have no idea. "We were one of your best teams and you know it, so why wouldn't we be close? I knew him better than anyone else on the team, I trusted him at my back. No matter what you mistakenly believed or felt was going on, it's your fault we almost lost everything."

"Don't change the subject." His gaze narrowed. "Is he Beckett's kid?"

She narrowed her gaze. "My son is off-limits, Michael. Last warning."

"You have to—"

"I don't *have* to do anything for you."

"I want my money back."

"Good luck."

He pointed a finger at her. "You took it, and I want it back."

She couldn't believe she was having this discussion when she was supposed to be planning a way to rescue her son. "You're determined to believe I stole from EGIS. Where did this happen and when?"

Lean fingers flipped open the file, then drummed on the tabletop. "I don't know why you want to play this game. The money disappeared the sixth of March. The year before you vanished. It was after the—"

"Operation in Nefta, Tunisia."

"So you remember."

She remembered. Indigo remembered everything. "We returned the second of March."

"Right, and my cache disappeared the sixth. You were the last one recorded going into the armory."

Her mind flew back to the date he accused her of pulling off the theft. But she hadn't done it. She'd spent the following week after the debriefing in a hotel with Beckett. A lavish place whose staff had an extremely hard time recalling who they'd seen there. Great for lovers who wanted a place to get away.

"Recorded? So you have me on video, then?"

"No, you know that. Your access code was the last entered."

"You're basing this on my access code? But none of the cameras picked me up. I wasn't there. I was at a hotel for a full week after our return. Being in an armory and stealing weapons and money would have been the last thing on my mind."

"Were you alone?"

"No."

"Who were you with?"

"None of your concern."

"So you're telling me you have an alibi but refuse to name him. Was it Beckett?"

She didn't flinch. "I'm not discussing my love life with you. You were my boss, not my father. Nothing will change that. You claim I'm a thief. I disagree. I have stolen, but because you told me to. I'm what EGIS made me, at times a thief, at times an assassin."

Two hours later, Michael stomped out, leaving her there. Five minutes later, Lisa came in.

"Let's go," she said.

On her feet, Indigo shuffled after the woman she used to work with. They didn't share words, just moved quietly along. Lisa took her back to a small cell with a tiny window in the door that offered minimal light. Removing the shackles, Lisa waited for her to enter, then closed the heavy door after her.

Damn. How was she going to get out of here now? She took care of her needs and stretched out on the bed. Closing her eyes, she allowed her thoughts to drift back to her son. How long would it be before she could hold him again? Chills broke out and she hugged herself, rolling to her side. She barely noticed the tear that trailed down from her eye.

Chapter Four

Beckett sat in the cafeteria with his chicken tenders and fries. As he flipped through the files Indigo had gotten from the mailbox—the ones EGIS hadn't absconded with when they captured her—he came across the image of Indigo's son.

Sean was a handsome boy. He had curly black hair and his mother's beautiful brown eyes and skin tone; it was slightly lighter than hers but still dark. Beckett stared at his features; in them, he could see himself. She hadn't lied. He had a son. His throat tightened, and he swallowed a few times. The picture was taken from his grasp, and he looked up to see Lisa's expression.

The blonde sat in the chair next to him, her hair drawn back in a French braid. "Did you tell Michael he's your boy?"

"No. How did you know?"

"Looks like the childhood picture you have of you and your sister." She nudged him with her leg under the table. "How do we save her? And your son?"

"What are you talking about? There's no way I can walk her out of here. Michael's forbidden me to go anywhere near her." He tipped his head and stared at her. "Why would you be on board with this?"

She reached into her bag and withdrew a file that she plopped before him. "In that case, let's try to figure out how Michael got the idea Indigo stole from him and how we clear her name. I have a feeling Iggy will be getting herself out soon enough."

He thought she'd be trying, as well. Also sure Michael would have taken that into consideration.

He opened the file and whistled low as he flipped through the numerous pages. "Where'd you get all of this?" A quick glance around proved the others meandering about weren't paying them any attention.

"My partner Marco's not the only one who's good with computers."

"We'd be seriously fucked if Michael finds out you're sharing this, right?"

Lisa shrugged and dipped some of his fries in mustard, then popped them in her mouth. "Who cares? Michael can kiss my ass. I'm doing it. You don't have to assist if you don't want to."

"Oh, I'll help. But I'm curious why you'd risk so much for her." He lifted his gaze from the sheets and looked back to Lisa.

She paused and took a long drink of her water then wiped the back of her hand over her mouth. "Do you remember that op in Tobago?"

"We thought we'd lost you after everything went crazy and blew up in our faces." Could that be the fuckup Indigo had accused Michael of today? But how had she known? She'd been long gone by then.

Lisa took a deep, shuddering breath. "I managed...I managed to get off one call."

He thought about how things had gone down after she'd been taken. Beckett had taken a bullet in the back and had been transported out. He woke in the States after the fact and discovered what happened later. Their boss had been unbearable. "Michael never mentioned a rescue operation. When I heard they sent your finger..." He trailed off.

"I knew the risks when I joined. I never expected EGIS to get me out." She rubbed the hand with her prosthetic finger.

"So, who was the call to?"

"A number I'd been given after my first op. A few days later, Indigo rescued me."

Beckett frowned. "How's that possible?"

"That's why I'll do whatever I can to try and repay her for her kindness and selflessness. She left her son, risked her life, and came for me."

He didn't have a clue of what to think or say about this. "I thought you two just tolerated each another."

Lisa's smile came easier now. "We did. I'd always been shocked about her giving me that number and quite honestly, didn't expect any help to arrive. But it did. *She* did. Indigo never asked questions, just managed to get me out of there."

Something else to talk to Indigo about. Beckett reached for some steak fries. "Let's get to work, then."

After eating and going over files with Lisa, Beckett returned to Michael's office. Julie sat there typing away. She turned pearl-gray eyes to him as he approached. All she did was tip her head toward the door, and he walked by and on into the office.

His boss sat behind his desk.

"Let her go," Beckett stated.

"We've been over this. I won't. And you shouldn't believe she has a son."

"Why not?" Sean was his; he was 100 percent positive of that.

Michael waved him to a chair. "I told you, women lie."

"So do men. She has no reason to lie about that."

"Wrong. She lies and gets your help. Do you really want to throw away everything you've accomplished on a lie?"

"You seem pretty adamant she's lying. How do you get to be so confident she isn't telling the truth? And what harm would it be to help her get the men EGIS wants alive?" He couldn't wrap his mind around why Michael was so set against helping Iggy. She'd been one of them. Her son, *their* son, deserved all the help EGIS could provide. He flexed his fingers into a brief fist before relaxing them. It wouldn't do to get worked up. That was part of Michael's MO, to get people to tip their hand. Besides, it was Iggy he had to confront about being kept out of Sean's life, not Michael.

"We'll get them without her. She stays locked up."

Beckett leaned back and placed an ankle on his knee. "The hard way. This would have been the perfect op. If she got caught, you could deny knowing her. Leave her to rot in another Mexican prison." He readjusted, leaning forward. "Which makes me wonder how you knew she was in *that* jail at *that* exact time. If you'd known her whereabouts during the last eight years, you'd have gone after her before now."

"Maybe she slipped up."

More suspicion tingled the back of his neck. "Doubt it. Who told you?"

Michael shook his head. "It was anonymous."

He frowned. "Which didn't set off any alarms?"

The man ate some sunflower seeds, dropping the shells on his desk. "No. We receive tons of tips."

"So what about this one made you decide to risk me on an op and find out if it was true?"

"It had been verified."

Beckett didn't like the sound of this. "How?"

"I had a visual conformation it was her."

"Has Marco checked out where the tip came from?"

"Tried and failed. Doesn't matter. I have her now, and I'm keeping her until she gives me back what she stole from me."

"She wasn't the one who took it."

Michael rolled his eyes and pushed away from his desk. "I don't need you to start on that bandwagon again. Her code. Hasn't been used since. It was her."

Why did Michael think Indigo would do something like this? "I was in the room listening. It wasn't her." Beckett considered confessing, but something stopped him. He realized he didn't trust this man. A hard pill to swallow after all the years he'd worked with him.

If he didn't trust Michael, what did that say about the rest of EGIS? Could he stay in a company with a director like this? But if he left, what would he do for a living?

"Your dedication and loyalty to a partner who abandoned you years ago is foolish. You should focus on the ones you can trust."

He was. And his gut told him he could trust Iggy. He

shook his head. "You're making a mistake, Michael."

His boss glared. "I'm done with this conversation. There's no option here for debate. You'd do well to remember that."

The situation was difficult to reconcile. Ever since he'd joined EGIS, he'd felt like they were his family. He'd trusted them, but now, his instincts screamed for him to free the mother of his child so they could rescue their son. Then again, if she stayed locked up, he could take care of the killings for her. He had the images and could get the gear needed. Unless the kidnappers expected only Indigo to accomplish the mission.

He held his tongue and sought the best way to make his point understood.

Whoop! Whoop! Whoop!

Both men bolted out of their chairs as the alarms began wailing. Their eyes locked, and Michael scowled. "Indigo."

His own thoughts had gone there as well, but Beckett was cheering for her to escape.

Michael punched a button on his desk and said, "I want her found. Do not let her leave these premises!" He leveled an accusing stare at Beckett, who held up his hands.

"I was with you, haven't spoken to her since the plane, don't even go there."

They ran from the room, past Julie, who, despite sirens blaring, didn't stop her work. The elevators took them down to the holding levels far beneath the earth. Weapons drawn, they exited. Men dressed alike prowled the halls.

"What happened?" Michael barked.

"We don't know, sir. One minute she was there, the next gone."

Beckett wheeled around and stepped back in the car,

punching the button for the ground floor. Years ago, Iggy had told him she'd found a way to bypass EGIS security and get out. As soon as the elevator doors opened, he hit the ground running, streaking past others heading for their posts.

Reaching the nearest SUV, he yanked the man out and slid behind the wheel, dirt whipping up from the spinning tires as he gunned the accelerator and shot off down the drive. Two other vehicles fell in behind him. At the end, he went left; checking his rearview, he noted one went right and the other crossed and hit the road nearly straight across.

Beckett parked a way off and walked to his destination. He needed to call EGIS in, but they'd just put her back in chains, and their son would be killed. He had money and could pull more before Michael realized what had happened. Most likely, he was killing his career with EGIS if he did this. He didn't care.

He leaned against a tree and waited. Thirty minutes later, the leaves rustled and a woman pushed into view. He waited until she took three cautious steps and moved by him.

"Hello, Iggy," he said, slapping a hand over her mouth and dragging her back, flush to his chest.

• • •

Indigo froze and allowed her body to fall limp. Beckett didn't flinch, he merely held her tighter.

"I'm not letting you go, Iggy. Nor am I taking you back. I have a car stashed up the road. It won't give us much time, but it'll buy some. Now, are you going to fight me or let me help you get our son back?"

She should've recalled it wouldn't work with him. Part of her wanted to resist him. Pound on him for the wasted time his carelessness had caused her. On the other hand, if he was going to help, she could use it. She stood on her own and he released her, clearly cautious of her reaction.

Crack! She delivered—in her opinion—a Rocky-worthy southpaw hit to his jaw, knocking him back.

"Fuck, that hurt."

"Good," she snapped. "Move it."

She struck out, leading the way, and he lit out after her. His long strides allowed him to catch her easily, and he reached the SUV the same time she did. She climbed in, immediately rooting around in the glove box. "Drive," she said.

He followed her instruction. After taking them to town, he paused at a bank and pulled up to the ATM. "I'm getting as much cash as I can."

She'd altered her position so she now hung over the front seat, pawing around in the back. Glancing over her shoulder, she found him staring at her ass, and she punched him in the shoulder. "Make it quick."

He did and pulled away as she finally sat properly.

"What are you looking for?"

"Weapons." She scrubbed her hands down her face. "He'll be sending someone after me." She slanted her gaze at him. "Unless that's you, and you're going to betray me again."

His rumble of anger filled the cab seconds before he slammed the brakes and skidded to a stop on the side of the road. "I did *not* betray you." He leaned close and gripped her chin in his strong fingers. His eyes blazed with anger.

"Really?" she retorted, unafraid of him. "I told you what would happen if Michael got a hold of me. He did, I'm guessing by your phone. Which of us was right on how that played out?" She curved her fingers around his wrist, adding her own pressure. "If something happened to Sean while I was in EGIS custody, so help me God, I'll make every last one of you pay." She shoved his hand away and pointed out the windshield. "We need to steal a car."

"Grand theft? Really?"

"Stop acting holier than thou, Beckett. Michael will wait to figure out how to best put it to the local LEOs, but we *know* he'll come after me." Michael didn't work well with the local law enforcement, but would if he had to.

"You have a plan?"

"How about some help?"

His gaze lingered on her, but she refused to acknowledge him, staring forward. They drove to a parking garage and parked on the fifth level. She hopped out and took off, only to have him clasp her upper arm.

"Together," he said, his voice a thread of dangerous warning. He reached into his pocket and tossed something at her. "Thought you might want this back. Maybe it will *help*."

It was the throwaway phone that had come in the packet. His sarcasm reminded her how wrong she'd been about him assisting her. "Fine," she bit off. "Thank you for getting the phone." She just cast her glance about, looking for the type of vehicle she needed.

"What about this one?"

She pivoted slightly to see what he indicated. A convertible. "No. Won't work." A small smile turned up her lips. "But the Bronco next to it…will."

It took them mere moments to break in, and after they'd

cleared out what they could from the EGIS vehicle, she climbed behind the wheel of the jacked-up SUV. She looked at him and beckoned with her hand.

"What?"

She repeated the motion, and he handed over his cell. It was a matter of seconds before she'd torn it apart, removed the tracking chip, and disabled the GPS. She'd been foolish not to do that earlier. Sure, she was rusty, but she couldn't afford any more mistakes. Tossing it back at him, she started their new ride, and drove out, turning away from town and heading toward the Everglades, Beckett beside her. Quiet.

"Tell me about him." He lowered his voice. "Tell me about my son, Sean." Beckett spoke his name in a way someone who'd never met part of himself did—reverently.

Her heart clenched at the thought of never holding Sean again. "Typical boy. Runs a lot, scrapes, bumps, and whatnot. He had a broken arm last year he got from flying from the tree house in the yard." Her right hand fingers lingered on the shifter. "He's inquisitive and enjoys building things."

Beckett smiled. "That was me as a boy. How's he doing in school?"

"He does well. Doesn't so much like the structured bit, but he's smart. He'd just rather be outside, getting dirty. He hangs out with a few boys. We came down to Puebla because he wanted to see the pyramids." She blinked back the threatening tears as she put them on the interstate. "This is all my fault."

He reached out only to pause and lower his hand. "Stop it. This isn't your fault. It's the bastards who took him."

"They took him because of *my* past. Things *I* used to do. I got out to keep this life from him, and it didn't even matter." Her voice was tortured.

From his expression, it was obvious Beckett wanted to comfort her but knew nothing he could say would make it better. For a moment, she expected him to say something anyway. But he didn't.

"Will you tell me where we're going?"

"The Everglades."

"For what? We need to get back to Mexico. And how the hell did you get out?"

She shifted into fourth and pressed the accelerator, keeping them in line with the flow of traffic. "I knew how to get out if I could get out of the cell. With Michael's hubris, it was fair to think he hadn't changed the security protocol."

"He will now," Beckett said, voice amused.

"Yes." She checked the mirrors. "So if I get caught once more, I'm fucked. I was lying on the cot after they'd taken away my meal tray and the door clicked open."

"Clicked open?"

"Yes. That sound when you break that air lock seal. That's what I heard, and I tested the door, then left. I have no idea who did it, but I wasn't about to stick around. The sirens sounded five minutes later. From your questions, I'll assume it wasn't you."

"Not me. I was with Michael. He'd told me I couldn't be around you."

"And you were thinking if you told him that Sean was your son he'd have a change of heart?"

"Michael isn't a bad guy, Iggy."

She noticed his hesitation in getting that out, but opted to keep it to herself. Beckett was finally questioning Michael and his motives. *Good.* It wasn't her place to push him to a decision, though. He had to reach his own conclusion or he might resent her for forcing the issue. "Never said he was. Just that unlike you, Beckett, I'm well aware of what lengths he'll go to in order to get what he's after. I don't have rose-colored glasses on when I look at him."

He began to protest, but she held up her hand. "You may as well sleep. It's going to take us a while to get where we're going."

The drive took them most of the night, because they did a lot of backtracking to ensure they weren't being followed. While EGIS was headquartered in Florida, as was her final destination, they were cautious. As she drove up the long winding road, she called on her memories to guide her along the correct turns, so they didn't end up somewhere in a pit of quicksand.

She pulled into the parking area and shut off both engine and lights. Dawn would be here in about two hours, although from the inky blackness, you couldn't tell.

"Where are we?"

"Come on," she said instead of answering.

Together, they walked toward the door of the house. *Never thought I'd be knocking on his door for assistance.* Her gut quivered, and she swallowed back her uncertainty. She wiped her hands off on her pants before she knocked. *Whatever it takes.* She'd do whatever it took to get her boy back.

Less than ten seconds later the door opened, and she stared into the lone eye of the black man who'd answered.

"Yes?"

"I need help. I'm in trouble."

"Figured as much for you to show up here. And with a

stranger."

"*We're* practically strangers. Will you help me or not?"

Silence thickened in the air. "Yes. You need to sleep first?"

"No, I need—"

"To sleep. I see it on your face. You're exhausted. Come back when dawn lights the world. You know where the small cabin is." The door closed in her face, and she gulped air trying to hold it together.

She didn't fight Beckett's support at her back.

"Who is that?" he whispered in her ear as they trekked across the dirt turning to mud with the rain that had just started.

"My father."

Chapter Five

A quaint but clean place. Beckett set their bags down in one of the cabin's two bedrooms. Sleeping arrangements would have to be decided later. Right now, he and Indigo needed to talk. A single lantern lit the living room, and the shadows weren't only in the corners—he saw them in her expression as well.

"You know you killed your career with EGIS by pulling what you did today, right?"

Shoving away from the wall, he nodded, walking toward her. "I know." Did he care? Nope. Maybe a little, but he'd take that up later. Could he work a desk job, punch a clock? There was also the possibility of him doing shit jobs at EGIS until he was once again in Michael's good graces.

Each step he took in her direction, she backed up until she ran out of room. He held her gaze and blocked her in with his arms. She swallowed, and he lowered his head. Slowly, making her damn sure she knew what was coming.

Him.

He didn't immediately take her mouth—no, he nibbled and licked at her lips, waiting until she opened for him. A whisper-like sigh escaped from her. Bombarded by the powerful emotions that never failed to raise their heads when he kissed her, Beckett wrapped his arms around her as the kiss turned primal.

His tongue surged forward into her mouth, and she met him, thrust for thrust, with her own. Pants growing tight, he wanted nothing more than to strip her of all clothing and relearn every single inch of her. Moving his hand down over her hip, he broke the kiss when she hissed and he felt something tacky beneath his fingers.

"You're injured?"

"I cut myself during the escape on something in the tunnel."

"Christ, woman, were you ever going to say anything?" He grabbed her by the wrist and tugged her down the hall to the single bathroom. "Get out of that shirt."

Muttering under his breath, he went to the bags in the bedroom where he'd dropped them, grabbed the medical kit, and returned. Life just wasn't fair at all. She stood there, shirtless as ordered, the whiteness of her bra slicing across her darker skin. Tempting him to all sorts of sin, but he had to focus on an injury.

It didn't matter that she wore a plain bra as opposed to something from, say, Victoria's Secret—it was a jolt to his system. Tearing his gaze away from her firm breasts, he focused on the wound above her hip.

He sat on the edge of the bathtub, turning her toward him, and got to work. "You should have mentioned this," he admonished as he cleaned it out.

"There are a lot of things I should have mentioned."

"This your way of apologizing for keeping my son from me?" He cleaned it methodically, not wanting to miss anything in the wound. It wasn't easy for him to suppress his anger. He remained furious at how she'd handled the situation. How dare she?

"Perhaps." She tensed slightly, and he paid closer attention to what he did, determined not to get distracted by the perfect form so close.

But it wasn't easy to ignore what was right before him. Full breasts, flat stomach, hips that…well, he knew well how they were in his hands as he drove into her, repeatedly, delivering them both to the highest planes of ecstasy.

"He's *seven*, Iggy."

"I know how old he is."

He blew out a frustrated breath and shook his head. Beckett teetered on the edge of control. He wanted to yell at her about Sean. Demand to be part of his life. Didn't he? Was he ready to be a father in more than just a name only? He focused on the task at hand. "Needs stitches."

"So do it."

It didn't take him long to thread the needle and hold it against her skin. There he hesitated. He hated this.

"Are you doing it or what?"

Glancing up, he found her watching him. Impatient. "Yeah."

Indigo didn't make a sound as he sewed her up. She stood rock still, barely breathing.

He needed to focus on something else. Other than her. Him. Not to mention the fact there were beds close by, which he *really* wished to make good use of with her.

"Your father can help us?"

"Yes. We may have our issues, but he'll help."

He finished stitching and tied off a knot. "What are we doing next?" With a blade, he sliced through the excess thread, freeing the needle.

"Get some sleep, then have him help with the number on the throwaway cell I got. If I'm lucky he'll be able to pinpoint the location it's coming from."

"Okay, and once that's done and we have Sean back, then what? New identities?"

"No!" Her adamant response made him look up at her. The lines of her face were set with determined resolve.

"Then we need to find who stole all that shit from Michael and clear your name so he's off your back."

She blew out a ragged breath and sat beside him on the edge of the tub as he began to put the medical supplies away. "You don't have to do this."

"Do you really think I'd leave you after everything we've been through? Besides, I know you didn't take it. We were in bed that week, and I'm damn sure you didn't leave it to travel to a different state to rob EGIS. I trust Michael, but this is bullshit. He's after something, you're right about that. And I'm not giving him anything else until we figure it out. I don't know why you didn't tell him about us."

She sliced her gaze to him. "It's none of his business who I was with. He likes to think he runs the world, but I'm not playing his games. Why didn't *you* tell him?"

"Figured he'd just think I was trying to cover for you," he said with as much nonchalance as he could manage. Spitting out anything more emotional would probably send her running for the state line. "You're exhausted, baby. Let's get you to bed." God, he wanted to hold her. Beckett wanted to comfort her, but nothing he could say would make it better. Well, he did have one surefire way he could distract her, but this was neither the time nor the place for that. Was it?

He stood, leaving the rest of the supplies there; he could put them away come morning. Reaching out for her hand, he did his best to ignore the pleasure something so simple as her touch brought him.

Without saying a word, he gave her a toothbrush and small tube of toothpaste and left her to take care of what she needed to. When she appeared, wearing her shirt again, he guided her to one of the two rooms and opened the door.

"Good night, Iggy," he whispered against her temple before kissing her lightly.

"Good night." She walked to the bed, and Beckett closed the door when she crawled onto the mattress.

He'd be going to bed with one raging erection. Wouldn't be the first time, however, and he checked outside to reassure himself all was secure. The woods were thick and everything black. The air was heavy with the promise of more rain, and he stepped back inside.

Part of him wanted to sleep in the room with her to make sure all was okay. Or the living room, to ensure that if something came in it had to go through him first. Logically, however, he knew if Indigo trusted where she was to sleep, he could as well.

Secure in that knowledge, he got himself ready for bed. Not much later, he crawled into the double bed, which was surprisingly comfortable, slid the Glock beneath his pillow, and closed his eyes.

He woke to the sound of heavy thunder. Opening his

eyes, he noticed the skies were dark. After swinging his legs out of bed, he padded to the door and stepped into the rest of the cabin. The house remained silent. He went across the hall to the other door and cracked it open, peering in.

She slept like the dead. His heart lurched at the sight of her exhaustion. She loved her son so much, because in her slumber tear tracks ran down her face. Backing out, he shut the door, leaving her to her much-needed sleep. He dug in his pocket for the picture of Sean he'd swiped from Indigo and sat on the edge of the couch. Christ, he was a father. That news had the power to rock him to the core. He skimmed his thumb along the edge, heart clenching as he feared the worst. Would he ever meet his son, his own flesh and blood?

• • •

Beckett spied her the second she entered into view, and he remained silent, taking the time to indulge his senses in her. He flexed his fingers around the cup in his hand, then released it to rest on the counter by the sink. Indigo walked out to the living room just as the first hint of light did its best to pierce the gloomy rain streaming from the sky. At the window, she paused and cupped her nape.

"I have to go talk to him."

"We," he corrected. "*We* have to go talk to him."

"Let's go." She walked to the door and, outside, was instantly soaked by the rain.

Once at the other cabin, she knocked and waited until her father opened the door. He wore what he had before and came across as put together as he had previously.

Once they stood in his entryway, Beckett stuck out his

hand. "Beckett Hanson."

"I know who you are." No handshake came. Beckett ignored the slight. Maybe if this were a different set of circumstances he would have insisted. But it wasn't. Everything was about Sean.

"I need you to track a phone for me," Indigo said.

"You arrive at my house, dragging someone with you in the middle of the night, to find a phone?"

Beckett waited, doing his best to allow her the lead on this. It wasn't anything that came easy to him. He wanted to be point. His body was hardwired to protect her.

She shoved her hands in the front pockets of her jeans. "Do you want to stand here and berate my actions or help me get your grandson back?"

There were many things he'd believed she would have said—that wasn't one of them. By the news, the man hadn't been expecting it, either.

"My grandson?"

"I don't have time to play games with you, Satchel. He was kidnapped, then I was taken when I was supposed to do some things to get him back. The clock's ticking."

Beckett watched him reach out a hand and wasn't the least bit shocked when Indigo gave the phone over. The two of them trailed Satchel down a hatch and on into a bunker beneath the house. Beckett gawked at all the equipment. How the hell did he have all of this beneath his home? Better yet, who the hell was this man?

"Give me a few seconds," Satchel said, then hit a few buttons, bringing the displays to life. He looked at them. "There's food upstairs. Go fix yourself something. I'll come up as soon as I have anything."

Beckett could taste her reluctance to leave, its thickness nearly overwhelming. Nonetheless, she allowed him to follow her up the metal steps to the main part of the house. He left the hatch open and accompanied her to the kitchen. He had two options here: talk about anything to distract both of them or kiss her until it led them to how they got Sean in the first place. Before he knew it, he'd stepped toward her, reaching for her arm.

• • •

"Want to tell me what the deal is between you and your father?"

Indigo paused and looked at him, a knife in hand as she waited for the toast. "Short version, ours is a strained relationship."

Beckett shoved a hand through his hair and groaned. "Strained? That's putting it mildly. I have so many questions I want answered on this, but later. Right now, we can figure out what the hell we're going to do next."

She let it go. There were things for them to work out on their own, and she wasn't thrilled with the notion of delving into her relationship with her father. Top that off with this thing with her and Beckett, about what was between them, or had been. She was so confused it was better if she kept focused. Forcing all emotion from her voice she said, "Fine."

"We need to get back to Mexico."

"I agree. But first, I have to contact them and make sure they still have Sean." Unease rippled through her like water. "And he's safe."

He clenched his jaw, and she waited for him to regain his own control. It had to be hard for him, too. Fighting to see a child you'd never met, before he was killed. "Lisa has been trying to find a way to get your name cleared."

The change in topic threw her for a second. Rather this than talking about her son and whether or not he breathed. "She shouldn't bother. I know it wasn't me, Michael knows it wasn't me. But he wants me blamed for it."

"Why?"

She took the toast, put two more pieces in for Beckett, and reached for the peanut butter. "All I know is when it happened we were shacked up in a hotel after a mission."

He faced her, one hand grabbing at her shoulder. "It may not work, but it could be worth a shot to tell him we were together on that date."

She lifted a brow. "You really think that'll work? We have a child together. He'll figure you'd say anything to help me because of that."

His expression grew serious, and he touched her cheek. "Not because of that. Not only."

Flutters erupted in her belly at the simple act, and she tried to ignore his words. He didn't make it easy. Not at all. The intense way he watched her, it made her feel…wanted.

Swallowing back her emotions, she spread the peanut butter then reached for the honey. "I have to find out when the money was taken, too. And how. Then I can figure out who did it."

"*We*, Iggy. *We.*"

"Why are you trying to clear me?"

He dropped his hand with a scowl and a muttered curse, then reached past her for another plate. "That's a discussion for another time." He turned his head, piercing her with his deep blue gaze. "Although if you really think about it I'm sure you'll figure it out."

She wasn't sure she was ready to think on it. Wasn't sure she was strong enough to deal with the answer. "It doesn't make sense. You never wanted children."

"You don't want to go there now, Iggy." Flames lit his eyes as he glared at her. "Lisa told me you were the one to save her."

Okay, that hadn't been where she thought the conversation was going. "She called."

"So you gave *her* a way to get in touch with you but not *me*." Disappointment rang through those words.

"I thought we weren't doing this discussion now?"

"No, we're not doing the one where *I* explain to *you* why I'm helping you. We're doing the one where *you* explain to *me* why you left without a word and no way of contacting you."

There was no mistaking the frustration in his tone now. She leaned against the counter and tapped her foot on the floor.

"I gave Lisa that number a long time ago and had honestly not given it any thought when I left."

"Didn't think of giving me a number at all?"

She'd thought about it, all right. "I did, but when I got to Snakes, Michael was there, and so I left."

An arrogant smirk lifted his lips while a gleam filled his gaze. "This has nothing to do with Michael, darling. This is about you running scared. Even before that night you'd been pulling away from me."

So he had a point. She willed her heart to slow down from his declaration and tried to ignore the throb between her legs. "We were partners. Shouldn't have been in a relationship, anyway."

"Perhaps not, but we were. An exclusive one. You know, the kind where we go without if our partner isn't there."

Jealousy filled her at the thought of him with other women. She licked her lips and forced herself to relax. "Good thing Michael told you that I bailed from EGIS. Then you could go get some really quickly."

His laugh was humorless. "Is that what you think of me, Indigo Grey? That I just went up and down the seaboard fucking my way with every whore I could find because I'm that much of a pig?"

She didn't have any answer to give. Shaking her head, she slid the plate in his direction. "Here."

"Answer me, damn you." His words were low and vibrated with dangerous anger. "Is that what you think of me?"

"I...I...what you do is your business."

She forgot how fast he truly was when he wanted to be, because he went from being across the space—which wasn't huge, but good sized—to in front of her in a blink. Every inch of him rigid. Fire brewed in his eyes as he stared down at her.

He touched the tip of her chin with one finger, and she froze as if he'd trussed her up in chains.

"Is. That. What. You. Think. Of. Me?"

"You're telling me you've been celibate for the nearly eight years I've been gone?"

"That wasn't my question." He moved closer and cocked his head to the side. "Have *you*?"

All she could think about were those firm lips moving over her skin. Delivering her to such ecstasy she didn't have any idea what else to do other than scream to the heavens. Licking her lips, she blew out a small breath. So close. All it would take to experience it again would be for her to lean in.

"Which question am I supposed to answer?" Her voice sounded breathless to her own ears.

"Both."

Her nipples tightened behind her bra, and the pulse between her legs became more insistent with each passing second. "No."

"No to what?"

She dug her nails into her palms and prayed for some strength, but he pushed nearer, not allowing her to get any purchase to shore up her defenses. "Both of your questions."

She needed a drink to get some moisture in her throat. Her fingertips burned with the desire to touch him, smooth over his muscled torso, enjoy each and every cut definition. The air crackled around them, and it wasn't solely from the storm that raged overhead. This had to do with the energy between them.

His scent surrounded her, intoxicating and euphoric. She longed to wrap it around her like a warm blanket and feel secure.

Beckett lowered his mouth until his lips were a hair-breadth from hers. "Damn, I've missed you, Iggy. So fucking much."

"Indigo." Another voice intruded into their bubble.

The tension surrounding them broke at that single word. Gaze locked with Beckett's, she swallowed. "Yes?" she called to her father.

"Come down here."

"I'll be right there."

Beckett's dark eyes smoldered. "This is far from finished between us." His words were low and full of promise.

She closed the small distance, covering the sides of Beckett's face with her palms. Thrusting her tongue in his mouth, she groaned at the familiar taste that hit her. Only one man tasted this good. Beckett was still for a second before he growled and took over the kiss.

Primal. Possessive. Intense.

The feelings and emotions she'd ignored since he blasted back into her life exploded, and she looped her arms around his neck, drawing his weight into her. This…this was how it should be. His heavy familiar weight pressing against her, the feel of his length against the seam of her jeans.

"No," he rumbled. "Not like this, Iggy. You told your father we'd be right there. Go."

It took a moment for his words to sink into her sex-charged brain. When he stepped away from her, she stood there a moment and tried to regroup.

What was wrong with her? This wasn't the time for this behavior. She was here thinking about sex—lots of it—when her son was in danger. What kind of mother did that?

Brushing by him, she headed for the steps. He didn't say a word, just followed her. She longed to run to him, wrap her arms around him, and have things how they were those nights they'd stolen together in hotels. Or under the stars.

Not going to happen. With a deep breath, she wandered down to where her father sat looking over the numerous screens before him.

"What did you find?"

"There are two people tracking this phone. Me, and this one who's not doing a very good job."

"EGIS," Beckett said, standing beside her, his arm brushing hers. "Marco said cloning the phone wouldn't work well, but Michael probably wanted you followed, regardless, when you…left."

"The original phone goes off, then comes on a day later. You won't be able to track him once he turns it off. He's smart and disables the GPS each time he shuts down."

Dread welled up again. "So how do you suggest I find them?"

"I'll monitor from here. When you get back to Mexico, call me on the phone right in front of you. I'll help you then. I've read a few text messages from the kidnappers, and they're looking for you. There is a number they also called that I dug out. I'm sure EGIS will get to it eventually, but right now I'll assume their attention is focused on tracking you down and not the other number on the phone." He turned in his chair to stare at her. "So both are after you. Be careful."

She shifted much like she'd done as a little girl. "This other number?"

"Is from the U.S."

She exchanged a look with Beckett. "Where in the U.S.?"

"Arkansas. It was only one call, and I traced it to a pay phone. I'll do some more digging on this end. You need to get to Mexico and rescue my grandson. Go on." He pushed up from his chair and shooed them up the steps.

He led them to his small garage, where he opened the door and dragged a tarp off a green Jeep Wrangler Sport, Sahara edition, soft-top, five-speed manual transmission with winch, fog lights, and thirty-three-inch wheels.

"Take it," her father said. "It's clean and will get you where you need to go. I'll get rid of the Bronco."

"Thank you," she replied. "Beckett, will you give me a minute?"

"Sure." He left her alone with her father.

She swallowed the nervousness in her throat and rocked back on her heels, suddenly unsure of what to say. Hallmark didn't make a card for "Sorry I've been out of your life for years and thanks for letting me intrude before I ask you to snoop into things so I can get your grandson back from the fuckers who kidnapped him."

"Bring him by so I can meet him when you get him back."

She took the keys he offered and gave a small nod. "I'm sure he'd like that."

"Go easy on him."

"Easy on who?"

"Beckett."

She tucked some hair behind her ear. "What are you talking about?"

He gave her a rare grin, softening his expression. "Daughter, that man is still in love with you." She stared as Beckett stood in the front yard, hands in pockets. He looked at her, and she beckoned him back over.

"Right," she said.

"You'll need him before this is over, Indigo."

Beckett climbed into the passenger seat. "Thanks for all your help."

Her father looked at him briefly, then refocused on her. "I want to meet my grandson."

"So confident this will work out?" She climbed in.

"Of course," he said. "My daughter isn't known for failing." He patted the hood and walked away without a look back. "And I don't expect her to begin now."

His confidence helped bolster her own. She wouldn't fail. Sean was counting on her.

Chapter Six

MEXICO

Beckett sat in the hotel room's only chair. He'd be damned if he let her stay alone. If a call came in, he'd be there to hear it. Rocking back in the chair, he propped against the wall—grateful the chair held him—and popped some gum as he watched her.

Indigo Grey sewed with severe concentration while he skimmed over her other purchases. Common everyday items that, in her capable hands, could become highly precise explosives. They'd also stopped and purchased more clothing on their way back down here. She'd managed to get a message off to the kidnapper, who was supposed to contact her once more.

She ignored him, although she'd check the phone at her side every few seconds, all without slowing in her sewing.

Her skin had a sheen of sweat on it; her hair was drawn

into a high ponytail, highlighting aristocratic cheekbones.

She was beautiful. Coldly so at the moment, and despite her being out of the game for years, this was the woman he'd trust at his back any day.

The ringing phone had him upright in a heartbeat. Their gazes met before she picked it up, and he hated the fear in the depths of hers.

"Hello?"

Beckett moved to her side, his own nerves stretched taut. How was she dealing with this? It was tearing him apart.

"In my room. Look, I was taken, *again*. I didn't exactly stand you up on purpose. My...my son, is he okay?" She made some noncommittal grunts before hanging up.

"What?" he asked the next second.

"Sean's alive. My weapons will be delivered in an hour. I'm on my way to get them."

"Alone?" Over his dead body. "Hell no."

"Not your call, Beckett. If they see anyone suspicious..." She shook her head. "No, I won't risk Sean. It's already putting this jackass on edge, what with me vanishing twice like I did."

Sean was his child, too, damn it. "Fine, but just so you know, I'm firmly against your plan, and I'll be following you after you go."

"I'm walking, so I need to leave now. I need time to think about things."

She dressed and left. He'd just slammed a new magazine home in his Glock when the door burst open. Marco and Lisa entered.

"Shit! What the fuck are you doing here?"

Lisa gave him a small smile. "I'm on vacation. What the

fuck do you think I'm doing here? I'm here to help. Just like Marco. Where is she?"

Beckett wanted to yell at them to leave, but Indigo and he needed help. "She's going to be pissed. She went to a place called Pollo Extraño. I assume there will be men waiting for her."

The Strange Chicken—what a name for an establishment. A low growl threatened to escape at the thought of her being injured or killed.

Marco said, "So let's do this. What do you need?"

"I need a place where we can stash the ones she's been ordered to kill. She's not keen on taking lives." Except maybe the one who'd kidnapped Sean. And Michael for risking her child again. "Michael said we need them alive, because they're important to EGIS. Indigo and I have worked out a plan to get them out of the way after it looks like she's killed them."

"Who's her kid's father?" Marco asked out of the blue after he sat on the bed and pulled up some areas on his computer.

Beckett stared at him. He held the image of Sean the kidnappers had stuffed in the envelope. "Why? Does it matter? He's a kid who doesn't deserve to be held hostage."

"Not arguing that, just thinking he looks a bit familiar." Marco stared at him with assessing brown eyes. Did he know?

Did Beckett really give a damn? "I suspect most kids look like their moms."

"Interesting response, which doesn't answer my question."

Beckett cocked a brow and steadfastly held Marco's gaze, not giving anything away. "Guess I don't think it matters. I'm heading out. Let me know what you find."

A taxi dropped him off near her meeting spot. He didn't go inside the restaurant, instead went across the street to the small café. Once seated at an outdoor table, he ordered *arroz con pollo*, a burrito, and a newspaper. He ate and read while keeping an eye on the place.

Two men hung around the entrance, constantly looking around, and he knew they waited for Indigo. After sending a text alerting the others of the tail, he took another bite of the rice. In between reading and eating, he sent pictures of the two guys to learn who they were. While he was glad Marco and Lisa had come to help, Indigo would be furious to see anyone else involved.

He'd just asked for another drink when she walked into view. She blended well, not standing out like a tourist. He struggled not to let the way her ass moved in those pants affect him.

Focus!

Unbidden, his mind drifted to how it felt in his hands, holding her as she was joined to him in the most intimate way. He smothered a groan as his body reacted to the trip down memory lane, hardening with readiness.

"She's in," he murmured via the earpiece to Marco.

"Got it."

Beckett waited for her to leave, but she hadn't come out by the time he finished eating. After settling the bill, he headed off up the street. He wanted to linger but couldn't risk it. His cell rang and he answered, pausing by a light post.

"She's heading your way." Lisa's coolly detached voice reached him.

"Thanks, hon. Can you see what I was looking for?"

"A rusty beige four-door sedan trailing her."

Shit.

"Got it." Placing the phone back in his pocket, he gazed up the street, pretending he was undecided where to go next. There she was. *Indigo.* Moving through the crowded streets as if she had not a care in the world. She saw him but gave no indication she knew him, her stride never faltering when she brushed by him. Despite craving to turn and watch her walk away, he didn't. Instead he continued on, crossing the street and tracking the beige car cruising slowly behind her.

Only when he was sure no one noticed him did he open his hand and unfold the paper she'd slipped in his grip.

Meeting Falco DeSalvo. Let me do my job.

His heart dropped to his feet. "It's Falco DeSalvo," he said to the other two.

"Fuck." Marco echoed Lisa's statement.

EGIS had been after DeSalvo for years. Every agency was after him, in fact. He'd always managed to slip away from their nets, seemingly with the ease of a magician. A terrorist who loved to flex his muscle and flaunt his freedom. He was also huge in the drug trade and sex-slavery rings.

"Drop back and let her do this," Beckett said, truly not giving a flying fuck if either of them heard his fear.

DeSalvo could snap at any moment, and he didn't want Indigo in the crossfire.

Be safe, Indigo. He waved for a taxi and gave his destination as he slid along the cracked leather seat.

God, how had things come to this? Less than seven days ago, he'd been on an op, focused, not dwelling over a past with a woman he'd loved. Now, she'd been tossed unceremoniously back into his life. Along with the news he was a father. Would she let him be part of Sean's life?

After paying the driver, he walked the remaining distance to the building across from the hotel and slipped into what had been designated op headquarters for the time being. Lisa and Marco were both there, kicking up the stifling heat even more.

"You sure Indigo's right about DeSalvo?" Lisa asked as she handed him a bottle of water. "Should we call Michael?"

Beckett shrugged. Taking a long drink of the tepid water, he wished for it to be anyone else. Anyone but Indigo Grey, who'd been out of the game for eight years.

"Of course, I'm not sure. But no way do we bring Michael in. Look what happened the last time."

Lisa said, "Michael would give her a shot at him first. It's DeSalvo. Then we help her to disappear once the op is finished."

More distrust of his boss reared its head. Despite his earlier confidence in Indigo's readiness, he shook his head. "No Michael. But Indigo's been out of the game for years. I worry whether she's sharp enough. And DeSalvo's a sneaky bastard." He rubbed the bridge of his nose. "I feel like we just tossed her into shark-infested waters, bleeding and without a life preserver."

"She's stronger than she seems, Beckett." Lisa reached out and placed her hand on his arm. "Does she know?"

He stared at her manicured nails with their pale pink polish. Indigo never painted her nails. "Does who know what?"

"Indigo. That you still love her?"

Grateful they were away from Marco, who worked on his computer, he furrowed his brow. "Still love her?"

Lisa's smile was sympathetic. "I watched you through 'nocs while you stared at her. It's not hard to pick up on, especially when you know the signs. For me, it's Michael." She shifted her gaze to the side at her admission. "I won't say anything, but you should tell her. She disappeared once, she can do it again."

Damn binoculars. "We'll see," he murmured.

"Get some rest. Nothing we can do until she gets back, anyway."

He headed to his room over in the hotel, the one adjacent to Indigo's, to wait. Not much later, he stretched out on a lumpy mattress and despite fighting to stay alert, closed his eyes, the lack of sleep over the last few days winning out.

The sun had set when he woke. Swiftly gathering his bearings, he moved to the door connecting him to Iggy's room. Voices muttered, and he cracked it open to see who it was. He didn't recognize them and sent a call to Marco and Lisa. He didn't want to wait for them to arrive as backup— he wanted to crash in to take care of the intruders. However, the small voice in the back of his mind reminded him this wasn't about him. When they announced they were in position, he kicked in the door, firearm drawn, and burst into her room.

. . .

The ride had been full of twists and turns in an attempt to disorient Indigo. Once they stopped, she'd been removed from the car and held still as hands ran over her body, checking for weapons. The man tsked in her ear as he drew the Glock from the back of her waistband. She never flinched despite wanting to face plant the bastard touching her with such intimacy. Some could make a pat down impersonal. This man...not so much. Her eyes focused, however, on the man sitting at a rickety folding table staring at her with a mixture of desire and amusement.

"You would come to me with a semiautomatic in the back of your pants?" He shook his head. "I think I am insulted."

DeSalvo. Why did it have to be him? Her heart thundered. "You weren't the one who spoke to me on the phone. Why not? And why would you be insulted? You want me to kill ten people for you in return for my son's life. Why wouldn't I have some kind of weapon?"

He grunted. "I wasn't going to be involved but after your capture, escape, capture again, and subsequent escape, it was important to meet you face-to-face. You have so many questions."

"That's all, Mr. DeSalvo."

"Thank you, Hector. Go get our guest a drink."

She wanted to refuse the drink, but she kept her mouth shut.

DeSalvo looked calm and collected as he sat there in a white silk suit. She, on the other hand, was sweaty and tired. She'd walked to two other places before the damn car that had been trailing her had finally picked her up, shoved a musty, dank bag over her head, and brought her here. An hour in the car with no air.

"Where are you staying?" he asked.

She told him, well aware he already knew. He directed some guys out there. "What do you hope to find in my room?"

"I want to see if you are working with anyone else."

"You threatened my son if I did, so I called in all of EGIS to help me out," she snapped.

He laughed indulgently. "Did you now."

"I want to see my son." She put the thought out of her head that the men would find someone in her room. Hopefully she'd eluded EGIS, and Beckett knew better than to come anywhere near her.

"Yes, your son. He is a very handsome little boy. I have three children of my own."

She blinked. "Congrats."

A heavy sigh. "You say that like you don't care."

"I don't. I want *my* son. And I want to know why you went through all of this to get me here. I've been out of this for years now. With all of your connections, you could find someone to walk into a room with all those you want dead and detonate a bomb. You have people who work for you stupid enough to do that."

"They are loyal."

"Call it what you will, it's stupid."

He tipped his head to the side. "And what about you? You are essentially doing the same thing."

"I have no plans on dying. I have every intention of getting my son back and raising him, watching him marry, and holding a grandbaby or two."

"Good to have plans. I have plans. Ah, here is Hector. *Agua fresca* today."

She took the drink offered by Hector. Her mouth watered when she took a sip. Watermelon *agua fresca*. Hardpressed not to drain the entire thing instantly, but she took a small drink.

He smiled at her as if reading her mind. "Drink, my

dear. There is plenty more where that came from." DeSalvo slipped off the table and gestured for her to follow him. She went, sucking on the straw and enjoying her drink.

"You never answered why me." They headed deeper into the building. From the outside, it looked like crap, but this man definitely knew how to live in comfort wherever he might be.

"Didn't I?" He paused and looked at her. "Would you care for me to answer that, or would you like to see your son?" Her expression must have given her away, because he gave a very unpleasant chuckle and continued on his way.

They pushed through some doors, and she paused, her feet cemented to the floor as she gazed over the room. Two men were in there, one at each door. In the center sat her son, playing a video game on a flat-screen television. Her lower lip trembled as she set her glass down on a table.

"Sean?"

He turned his head, then dropped the controller and jumped to his feet. "Mama!"

Arms wide-open, she fell to her knees and embraced him. For a moment, nothing else mattered. Not the fact they were in danger, not that one of the world's most wanted terrorists watched them, nothing. Her son was safe.

"I missed you, Mama."

She kissed his forehead and gave him a smile, in spite of longing to cry and hold him tighter. Never letting him go.

"I missed you, too, baby. So much." She smoothed some hair back from his face. "Are you okay? Are they treating you good?"

He nodded. "Can I come home now, Mama?"

The words had to be forced past her lips. "Not yet, baby.

Mama's still working, but when I'm done, I'll come for you and we'll go home together. For now, you need to stay with them."

"Is that why you're so dirty? You've been working?"

"Yes." She cupped his cheek, fighting back the tears. She'd thought she'd lost him. She held him close again, her legs too shaky to stand. Plus, she just wanted one more second with him.

"Come, Indigo, it is time for us to have our discussion."

She tensed at DeSalvo's voice but wasn't going to risk pissing him off. "You listen to these men and don't cause them any problems. But I want you to never ever forget something," she told her son. Brown eyes looked at her and waited. She hugged him tight again. "Never forget how much Mama loves you. Never."

"I won't."

"I love you, Sean." She stood and reluctantly moved back from him.

"Love you, too, Mama."

More liquid burned at the corners of her eyes. "Go play." He spun around, and she forced her legs to carry her from the room. The moment the door shut behind DeSalvo and her, she spun on him. "You hurt him, and there won't be any place in this world you can hide from me."

"I've always enjoyed your feistiness, Indigo. But don't mistake my goodwill for weakness." His voice hardened.

"I'm not mistaking anything. I know exactly who and what you are, DeSalvo. Let's get this chat done so I can get my weapons and get your goddamn job over with. I want my son, and I want you out of my life forever."

His smile caused her skin to crawl as if she'd been

dropped into a pit of snakes. *Pull it together, Indigo. Don't let him know he's getting to you.* She'd done this before, faced down scum like him, and persevered. Never mind she'd been out of this life for years. Sean depended on complete success.

She blinked and slid to a chair. "You wanted to talk, so talk."

One of his men provided them with more drinks. She took hers and indulged, all the while tracking DeSalvo as he lowered himself into a leather chair, facing her. She wanted to kill him now, then take her son and leave.

"You have the list. You will not see your son again until it is over. I didn't want to let you see him this time, but I figured it would be the best way to get your cooperation, given our…lapse…in time. In fact, so you do not think to attack, he is not here any longer. My men took him elsewhere the moment we left the room."

"You'll have it. Why did you pick me? And why, if you wanted me to do this, did you have me put in a jail a few hundred miles away from here?" No matter how much she wanted to, she couldn't blame DeSalvo for Michael taking her to EGIS headquarters.

A tightness appeared around his mouth, lasting no more than a flash, but it was enough. He wasn't in charge. Someone else had something over him. He tugged on the sleeve of his pristine suit coat. "That," he said. "That was unfortunate. Had you just accepted your son being taken, the real cops wouldn't have appeared." A shrug. "A minor snafu."

"And the men on the road who tried to run me off? Was that another *unfortunate* snafu?"

"Mexico is a dangerous place, my dear. Things happen all the time."

His words might have been collected, but his expression didn't follow suit. She had more confidence he wasn't top dog. Which meant there were more players. A fact she'd look into once she got out of here. Right now, she had to remain focused on the killer across from her. Lord, she hated this life. So much damn subterfuge.

"So they do," she agreed.

His grin was unsettling.

"I won't even ask why you want these people killed, but I want to know why you want *me* to do them. And you want me to kill them all? Not anything else? Like having them arrested?"

DeSalvo frowned. "Dead. Not breathing. No longer living. You will do as I say."

"I understand the concept. Dead." She leaned forward, struggling not to jump across the distance and wrap her hands around his neck.

"Listen well, Indigo Grey." His tone grew dangerously silky, a panther rising and setting his sights on his prey.

A few hours later, with another drink nearby, she stared over the array of weapons he'd gotten for her. The man had pull; there were things in the collection she'd not asked for. Taking a large duffel, she opened it and began loading what she needed. The door burst open, and two men hastened in.

If she killed them all, what were the chances she could make it to Sean before someone put a bullet into him? Provided he was even in the building. Not good, so she continued loading the bag.

"What did you find?" DeSalvo's voice was the smoothest of cognac.

"No one else with her, but her room had been robbed.

We got there in time to see the police dragging two men away. But no EGIS. Or any other agency."

"Interesting."

Great. All her purchases could be gone. She took a deep breath. Nothing she could do about it here and now. Also meant they didn't know about the Jeep, so she'd have some things there. Focus on one thing at a time. She finished loading the bag.

"Not much more than one week left, Indigo Grey." DeSalvo gave her a wad of cash. "Some targets may be in other places in Mexico."

She flipped through the roll. He funded his murders well. Distaste welled up in her stomach as she realized she *was* like the others who worked for him. Who's to say he wasn't holding one of their loved ones while they did what he wanted?

Head confined in a sack, she rode in the backseat while they took her on many turns until letting her out of the car and tossing the bag at her feet.

Darkness had long since fallen by the time she lugged the duffel stuffed full of weapons up the three flights to her vandalized room. Unlocking it—the front desk had told her they replaced the old door and had given her a new key— she pushed in and turned on the light.

She found her things put away and knew that had been Beckett. After securing the door behind her, she set the bag down on the floor beside the bed. Lord help her, she just wanted to catch some z's. It wasn't meant to be, however, because the connecting door between her room and Beckett's opened.

He stood there wearing the hell out of his jeans and

tight tee. His gaze raked her up and down, as if confirming she was okay.

"What?" she snapped.

He moved like lightning, and she found herself in his embrace, the wall at her back with Beckett at her front, pressing into her. His mouth descended on hers much as it had at her father's house. Harsh and demanding.

She opened beneath him, welcoming his touch. Their teeth clashed, tongues dueled and danced with each other. His hands crept up her shirt and covered her breasts.

Legs trembled at the contact, and she whimpered, pushing into him, begging for more. He spun them around and they crashed into the wobbly table, knocking it to the floor. It didn't matter. Against another wall, she hooked a leg around his hip and ground into him. Flames arced between them, and he tore his mouth away and began lifting her shirt when the door opened.

They sprang apart. Indigo drew her firearm, only to blow out a shaky breath when Lisa and Marco entered. This was the place they'd relegated as their ops room, and they all had keys for it. Always helpful when a hotel still used actual keys.

She glared at Beckett and read in his gaze his desperation that she trust him one more time and not blow all of them away. Indigo knew she shouldn't have been so jumpy, but she hadn't fully settled back into the role of agent. It chafed that Beckett hadn't been surprised when they walked in. Even a little. He could have been as lost in the kiss as she'd been and not paid attention. She pushed the thought away. It didn't matter. This couldn't happen again.

"This will be continued." Beckett moved closer and

whispered in her ear as she returned her weapon to the back of her pants.

Why the hell didn't they do anything normal? They'd always been hidden away together in some foreign country. The one time they'd tried for a normal date was the time she'd never showed. Despite the circumstances, sex with him would have been awesome, and she could have used the relief.

"Fill us in on what happened," Lisa demanded.

She cut her gaze toward Beckett once more. His face gave nothing away. Not to anyone other than her. She watched the tic in his jaw. His whispered promise came back to her, and she swallowed before lifting the table back up. It wasn't broken. They'd done that, too. Broken a few tables in their escapades.

Lisa continued, "I swear, we're here to help. You've never met Marco, but he's been with us for a long time."

Marco introduced himself. The man was from Tegucigalpa and had been an old friend of Michael's before joining EGIS five years ago. He moved to her side and stared down at her. "I'll take your phone to my room and see what I can get from it."

She shook her head. "No. It doesn't leave my side. Go get what you need and come back here. I'm not parting with it. I don't know what you hope to find on it. It's a drop phone. Their number isn't going to lead you anywhere."

"Help me out here, Beckett," Marco implored.

"You really think he'll make me give the phone to you?" She glared at Marco. "He can't. This is my only lifeline to *my* kid."

"Go get your shit, Marco, and stop flirting." Beckett's

order was sharp.

"Was he this bossy when you worked with him?" Marco asked with a wink.

"Even more so," she said conspiratorially, feeling more at ease with him. While she was upset Beckett had brought in others, she couldn't ignore how nice it was to have their assistance.

"Figures. I'll be right back." He went to the door. "You two kids behave now." Marco slipped out.

"Do you have to flirt with everyone?" Beckett asked her once they were alone.

"Yes. It's hardwired into my DNA. You know, like yours of being an ass."

Chapter Seven

Indigo's brief glance at Beckett informed him she remembered all their times on tables that had nothing to do with anything other than pleasure between them. Her pupils dilating and the slight nostril flare had been dead giveaways. Smirking, Beckett leaned against the wall and perused the woman who had everyone's attention while she told them about her encounter with DeSalvo.

Tan cargo pants and a white tee were stained with both sweat and dirt. Her hair was coming free from her ponytail. Granted, some of that had been from him as he kissed her.

He'd heard her return and come over to see how she was doing. All his intentions vanished when he'd seen her standing there looking so damn hot and lost. He'd been so worried all he could do was touch and kiss her as if to prove to himself she was there. One thing led to another, and he was more than ready to take her against the wall when the door opened. Forcing his mind from much more pleasurable pursuits, he cleared his throat, only to be sucked right back into the vortex of the firestorm that defined his relationship with Indigo Grey.

"Why did he want you?"

Lisa's question drew his mind from the feel of Iggy's lips on his, her tongue sparring with his.

"He never told me, constantly avoided that question. Just said he wanted my skills." She crossed her arms, drawing his attention, briefly, to her full breasts.

"He does know you've been out for years, right?" Beckett asked, determinedly keeping his gaze on her face.

"Yes. He just said I'd remember all of it if I wanted to see my son again."

Beckett bit back a curse. He hated their son was the pawn in this. They couldn't plan an all-out assault unless they knew where he was, for fear of hurting the child.

Marco returned to the room and took up a place along the wall. Time for him to come up with a contingency plan, in case this all went south or DeSalvo reneged on his agreement.

Indigo sighed and rolled her shoulders. "He's mobile. Living in comfort but mobile. They have generators for power, so even if I knew where he'd taken me, I'm sure they are gone now." She paced a few steps before leaning on the wall he'd just had her against. "He's jumpy. I noticed about thirty armed guards hanging around."

"What else did you two talk about?" Marco asked.

Indigo shook her head. "Nothing."

Okay, now she was lying. Beckett would bet his life on it; the question was why?

Marco apparently didn't buy it, either. He glowered at

her but held his tongue. "Are you sure? You were gone an awful long time to not talk about anything else."

Her gaze, sharp as razors, cut into the man. "I don't expect you to believe anything but what you want to. I don't know you, and you don't know me. I'm telling you how it was. Look, I have to start killing people in the morning, and I'm running really low on sleep, so if you don't mind."

"You've worked on less sleep before." Marco made the observation. "You were an agent."

She arched a brow at him. "Exactly. *Were.* I haven't done this for years." She took a step toward him. "And if it's all the same to you, I'd really rather have decent sleep beforehand so my son doesn't suffer for my mistakes." She undid her ponytail and shook out her hair. "You do this all the time. Me? I'm in the PTA, and I bake cookies now. Something I'm pretty damn good at. However, in the past few days, I've seen my son kidnapped, been tasered a few times, thrown into a jail where they enjoyed beating me, jumped from a moving vehicle, been shot at, and was almost driven off the road. Today, I've spent too much damn time with my head inside some stank-ass bag so I didn't know where I was being taken. I'm tired. I'm fucking exhausted. Let me get some sleep."

Beckett wanted to kick each and every one of them out, himself included, but he remained frozen where he stood. He'd be damned if he left. Marco handed her a packet then returned to stand beside Lisa.

Lisa gave Beckett a pointed look. He nodded. With Lisa and Marco here, he wouldn't put it past Indigo to try and give them the slip. Worked perfect with his plans for her.

They left, so it was only Beckett and Indigo in the room.

She gazed at him with a weary expression, then turned and plodded into the small bathroom. The shower kicked on and he groaned, sitting down in the chair. A short time later, she reappeared wrapped in a towel and nothing else.

Powerful need rocketed through him, shaking him to the core. All of her skin scrubbed clean, and he couldn't help envisioning what he knew to be below that damn lucky terry cloth. Clenching a fist, he struggled to stay seated and not go to her.

Indigo barely acknowledged him. She grabbed some clothes and vanished back into the bathroom. When she came out this time, she wore a cropped shirt and some shorts. Did it help his libido? Nope, not in the least.

"I take it I have you here through the night," she murmured.

"Yes."

"So want to explain to me why you brought in Lisa and Marco?"

She grabbed the folder of pictures and carried it with her to the bed, where she sat cross-legged. The springs squeaked slightly. He knew exactly how loud they'd get if he were to join her there. Especially if he was to lower himself between her thighs or she was to climb on him, they would... Oh, no, this wasn't productive. Time to get something else to focus on. And thinking about sharing a bed with her every night for the rest of their lives wasn't it. Back to the task at hand.

"Because we're going to need the help. Don't bother denying it."

She grunted and tapped the pencil on the paper.

"What are you doing?"

"Figuring out the best order to take them in. Something I wanted to do today, but was a bit occupied."

He moved to sit beside her. She had a legal pad, and he took in what she wrote. "Marco came through with the priorities of these men, then."

"Yes, why they're wanted by EGIS, along with their connections and locations—they're scattered over a few cities here in Mexico. Most are drug lords, cartel members, and the like. Marco's really good with a computer."

Ignoring the spike of jealousy he got at the admiration she had for Marco, he nodded. "Man can find just about anyone. Or get you anything."

"He said he was tracking the weapons I got as well."

"Yes, it'd be good to get someone who supplies terrorists off the streets."

"But I doubt it's going to make much of a difference."

Lord, she smelled so good. Fresh and clean, like the soap with a hint of her scent. She'd always smelled delicious. Staying away from her was going to be harder than he thought. So much harder. *Just accept it, Hanson, you're fucked.* Royally, deeply, and most assuredly fucked. Like he needed the reminder.

"Why? Each one we get off the street helps."

"There are five more waiting to replace the one removed, Beckett. You know that."

"You're cynical."

Her laughter was harsh. "There's always someone looking to make a name for themselves. So, yes, I'm cynical. And I'm more than that. I'm a mother who'd much rather be holding her son, reading him a story, and tucking him into bed."

She made a list on the paper, her pencil strokes sure, placing the order in her short cursive.

He wanted to offer comfort, but she radiated a *keep away* look. "We'll get him back. Why don't you tell me what you lied to Marco about? You and DeSalvo talked about something else. What was it?"

The lead broke on the paper as her hand shook. Beckett reached out and took both the mechanical pencil and paper from her, setting it to the side and gathering her close to him. To hell with her being standoffish and isolated.

"He's trying to be so brave, but I know he's scared. He asked me to take him home, and I couldn't. I *couldn't*. I had to leave my son there. Now I have no idea where he is." Her words were so soft he almost didn't hear them, but there was no way he couldn't understand the agony in her voice.

The realization hit him. "You saw him?" His words were shaky. Adrenaline hit him square, his heartbeat raced. Even so, dread accompanied his elation at her news. An ache took up residence in the back of his throat, combined with anger at being kept out of the loop of knowledge on his child. Something else he had to ignore now—him yelling at her about that wasn't anything but counterproductive.

Her lithe body trembled beneath his. "Yes. That's what we talked about." She blew out a harsh breath and pushed away from him. "I can't…can't do this."

"Accepting comfort doesn't make you weak, Indigo."

God, he would give his life to wipe the devastated look from her face. Give her back her son.

"My son doesn't have anyone to comfort him. I'll allow myself to break down once this nightmare is over." She reached determinedly for the yellow pad he'd just taken from her. "Let's figure this out."

Her final wall snapped into place, and he let it go. They

worked well together, and their time apart hadn't changed that. It didn't take them long to figure out the order and locations each man would be taken from. There would be more planning, of course, but that would come later.

"Murders are common here, so the cops shouldn't make too much of a fuss until I get closer to the end of the list. Given that Marco can't find any connection between them, no one will see a pattern. Aside from these two," she said, tapping the paper. "They've been seen at the same strip club from time to time, but nothing that suggests they're exchange-Christmas-gifts type of close. But clubs like this are rarely well lit, so I could do two in the same place. Not a fan of that idea, but it could be done."

He nodded. "With pictures taken of each pretending they're dead, it should convince DeSalvo."

"I hope so. I might have been an assassin at one time, but I hate to kill for real anymore." She ran the lead point of the pencil down the sheet. "I have to plan for some poisonings, a few shootings, a stabbing, a car accident, and a work accident." Her tone conveyed her reluctance.

"Then we can use Lisa and Marco to keep them confined while you carry out the rest of the missions. I'm assuming you want to do different ones to keep the cops from thinking there's a serial killer in the area."

"Yes. I don't want the cops on my ass as well. Do you think Marco will be able to keep them quiet? I know Lisa will, but is he okay?"

"Marco can do his job. The men aren't going to be happy being held, but better that than dead."

He stared at her face and couldn't help reaching out to touch her cheek. She slanted her gaze to him, and for a moment, it was nothing but the two of them. Then she returned her attention to the list and made a copy. They'd have to be near the victim in order to handle cleanup, hold them somewhere safe and secure until the entire op had been completed.

"Do you remember Calais?"

Of course he did. Calais was a town in northern France. "We were after a couple of hit men. They had some targets who'd be at Place d'Armes." He smiled with the memory. "We stayed at the Hôtel Meurice de Calais and attended the monthly dinner and dance cabaret at the Rue Royale and the 555 Club."

An almost wistful smile turned up the corners of her lips, softening her expression a hundredfold. "I was thinking of the mirror hanging on the wall when we first got there. Do you remember? The large, ornate one."

He furrowed his brow as he tried to recall the mirror. Watching her, he noticed how she kept working on the paper in her lap. The only mirror they'd discussed had a bug in it, and they'd known someone had wanted them monitored. They'd never removed it, just passed notes when necessary, or turned up the radio, or spoke in the bathroom with the shower running to cover the noise.

"Yes, why?"

"I remembered staring at your reflection and wondering how it was you weren't married. You were an amazing agent, Beckett. Still are, from what I can see. Anyway, I promised myself that day I'd do everything I could to be the best partner I could to you. I know it's late and probably doesn't mean spit, but I am sorry about just disappearing on you like that. Truly, I am."

Beckett didn't speak for a few moments. He knew what it cost her to say that. She'd alerted him to the fact the room was bugged and admitted what she'd done to whomever was listening—probably Marco. Hell, perhaps both of them.

Their gazes locked, and he reached out with one hand, cupped the nape of her neck, and drew her closer to him. With infinite gentleness he brushed his lips along hers, capturing her butterfly-like sigh.

"Think we could start over?" he asked, moving away from her all too tempting mouth. "Maybe pull this off without killing each other."

This time she approached him. The notepad slid silently to the floor as she leaned closer and kissed him. He struggled to stay motionless and let her set the pace, a decision he was hard-pressed to keep when her tongue slid into his mouth and stroked along his. His pants were uncomfortably tight, and he bit back his moan. She drew back and stared in his eyes.

"I'd like that." Her words were soft yet heartfelt. "I need to get some sleep. Would you like a pillow? I'm assuming you're sleeping here tonight."

His body ached for hers, yet he rose from the bed and slipped through to his room to get some things for the night. It didn't take long, and he returned. She'd put her hair up in a wrap, and he smiled as he touched it. Camouflage. She did always love her camo.

He so wanted to ask her questions about their son. About her. About what would happen once this was over. He wanted to be part of Sean's life. But that was a discussion for another time. Without eavesdroppers. He fell into a restless sleep in a chair and bolted up when a hand touched his arm.

"Shh," she whispered in his ear. "This can't be at all comfortable. Come to bed. Not sure why you didn't just join me in bed to begin with."

His body tightened at that suggestion as he followed her. He'd taken the chair because he wasn't so sure he would have been able to restrain himself from indulging in her. The springs squeaked again as he lowered his weight on them. Seconds later, Indigo curled up against him, her head on his shoulder and her arm around his waist. They covered up in a light sheet and he closed his eyes, her scent in his nose. The warmth and familiarity of her form pressed to him made relaxation come so easily. Turning slightly, he brushed his lips along her forehead and fell asleep with Indigo where she belonged. In his arms.

He woke alone and fought the urge to bolt up, weapon in hand. *Indigo.* Where was she?

Heart slowed immediately as he spied her. She worked at the small table, one leg propped up on the seat beside her, head near her knee.

She looked delectable. Not at all like the assassin he knew her to be. Was this how she looked at home? Did she enjoy her morning tea as she watched the sunrise? He wanted to be part of that life with her. What did he know about a normal life? Was he ready to give what he knew up for her and the son he'd yet to meet?

The curtains were drawn. But some of morning's first light sneaked in, adding a soft glow about her. She wrote furiously—the sound of the pencil scratching on the paper had woken him.

He climbed from bed, went to the bathroom, and took

care of what he needed to. After washing his hands, he stared at himself in the mirror. What was he doing?

She'd barely been back in his life a few days, and he was just as lost as he'd been before. *Get a grip, Beckett.* He was here to do a job. Nothing more. He was an EGIS agent. He was also a father.

Would she let him be in Sean's life? His expression hardened. She had a fight on her hands if she tried to keep him away from his own flesh and blood. He took several deep breaths and left the room.

Back out in the main room, he walked up to her side and peered over her shoulder. He recognized the schematics immediately. She'd broken down almost everything.

"You've been busy. Why didn't you wake me?" He trailed a hand along her shoulder.

"You looked like you could use more sleep." She reached among the papers and handed him three. "These are for today."

"Three? You want to take out three?" He shook his head, disbelief mounting. "In one day?"

. . .

Did she? Nope. Would she? Hell, yes.

She'd known the moment Beckett had woken and forced herself to not look at him. Waking in his arms had been a dream she'd wished would continue forever. It had been so long since she'd felt that way. Safe. Secure. Protected.

She'd watched him sleep, memorizing the planes of his face. Harsh. Masculine. And perfect. His five o'clock shadow would feel so good against her skin—it always had before.

Full lips never failed to set her on fire.

Cursing herself for allowing the luxury of lust while her son was scared and alone, she'd gotten up and gotten to work. Now Beckett stood next to her, fresh from a shower and offering all kinds of temptation. Her slit clenched with a need no other had ever been able to create within her.

"I don't have much choice. I have to get them out of the way and focus on the ones who'll be harder. Then again, maybe I'll just do two." She jotted down more notes. "Do you know where you'll keep them? They need to be completely off the grid until this is finished and I get Sean back. If even one of them escapes and DeSalvo learns that I haven't been doing what he wants…" She shook her head, not wanting to go there. "I just wish I knew why he wanted me."

Beckett gave her hand a short squeeze. "We have a secure location picked out. They won't be discovered, Indigo. Marco and Lisa will do their part. They went there yesterday to ensure it's safe."

"So they're no longer in the building across the street?" His hesitation made her laugh, although there was little amusement in it. "Never mind, I know better than to ask. Do what you got to do."

He placed his hands on her shoulders, and everything in her responded. Cells migrated toward him, knowing the pleasure he brought her. She reprimanded her traitorous body, but to no avail. It knew what it wanted, and that was Beckett. All he had to do was be in the room with her and she was drawn toward him. Both physically and mentally. Her skin tingled with anticipation of his light caresses. The way his fingertips trailed along her curves. Her gut tightened at the memory, and she swallowed the large lump in her throat. Her body grew slick with readiness, and she fought the need to squeeze her legs together. Not what she needed to think about right now.

"Are you hungry?" he murmured against the skin of her neck.

Dear Lord, please, please, please *give me enough strength to deal with him.* Words didn't form, and it took her a few attempts before she was successful. "Already ate."

"You left?" The question was harsh.

She breathed in relief. This Beckett—while fine as hell—she could deal with much easier, his demanding self as opposed to the sensual and all-too-seductive one who could charm the devil out of his kingdom if he wished.

"I walked all the way over to one of the bags from yesterday." She shook her head. "I know what I'm supposed to do, Beckett. Don't yell at me." She pointed to her notepad.

"Poison?" Beckett questioned from behind her, then sat in the chair beside her.

"Why do you sound so shocked? I've used this method before. We both have. This concoction sends the victim into a catatonic state simulating death. If he's administered the antidote in time, he'll have a full recovery. Both Lisa and Marco will have it on their person since I don't know—nor do I want to—who's going with him to your location. The man will be fine."

She carefully added three drops from the small vial on her left to the petri dish before her. Beckett picked up another dish and began making more for her. The ease with which he assisted helped calm her.

Picking up the ring she'd wear, she opened the stone on the top and filled the hole with an eyedropper. She pressed the pressure points on the sides of the ring and smiled when the thin needle peeked out. With her free hand, she swiped a paper towel and held it to the tip of the needle, pleased when it showed signs of moisture.

The ring didn't activate unless there was equal pressure on either side, so only when she pressed her fingers together would the hairlike needle slip free and administer the poison.

After she'd cleaned up from that, she fixed the blood pack to make it look like she'd killed the other man she had plans for today. A couple other items and she'd be ready for him as well.

Beckett asked, "How's it coming?"

"What do you think of this consistency?" She pointed at the blood pack. "I don't want it to smell too sweet, because I'm not sure who else will reach the body."

He lifted it and sniffed. "Add a bit more iron, I'd say about another dropper full, and you should be fine."

She did and filled the empty bag. "Hold this for me," she said, handing the pack to him.

"Just hold it?"

She lifted her gaze to his, and he grinned. They stood, and he tossed her the pack. They moved to opposite ends of the room and then headed toward one another. Starting with her hands in her pocket, she accidentally bumped into Beckett then kept on going.

He spun around to face her and opened his coat. "Placement is good. I barely felt you."

She frowned. "*Barely* felt? That's not good. You shouldn't be able to feel me at all. Let's go again." He pulled the packs free and launched it back to her. She snatched them from the air and took a deep breath. "Okay, once more."

Once more turned into five more attempts. With a frustrated groan, she slumped back in the chair. "I've lost my touch," she said.

"No, you haven't." He began filling the other packs for her.

"You said each time you could feel me putting it on you."

"*I* can. You haven't lost your touch, though, Iggy." He pinned her with his gaze, the intensity burning her. "There's no way in this world you could touch me and I wouldn't know it. This guy won't know a thing."

· · ·

Four hours later, Indigo smiled at the waiter who'd delivered her order of *queso flameado*. She was famished. The place was a dive on the outside, but the inside wasn't half bad. For a strip club. She had a room secured at the hotel and had taken care of the setup for the first three targets. Number one would be here soon. She had left a note for them to bring Diego Garcia to her table when he arrived and sat in the back.

She ate swiftly and ignored the main stage, where women gyrated around poles and humped the polished wood hoping for tips. Utilizing this time, she centered herself, shoving back the last of her nerves. She'd done it before and could do it again. Just like riding a bike.

"He's here," she muttered as she washed down her final bite with some bottled water. She didn't touch the bud in her ear; it felt so natural to her. He strode in her direction, and she pushed to her feet, holding out her hand. "Senor Garcia, it is good to see you again." She adopted a Brazilian accent.

His hand tightened around hers, and she ignored the sweat-slicked palm as he placed a sloppy kiss on the back. "You are beautiful. We have met, you say?"

She gestured for him to sit and watched as he carefully slid his bulk into the booth. "*Sí.* I am not surprised you don't remember. There was so much else going on at that party and we only had a brief introduction."

"I wish I had paid more attention to you." He reached for her hand again. "Let's order some wine."

"That would be lovely. I apologize for eating, but I hadn't had anything all day."

His thumb rubbed the inside of her wrist. "Perhaps I could persuade you to partake in some dessert?" He made the word disgusting and lewd. The guys listening in would be laughing or rolling their eyes. Were she on the other end, she would have been.

This was pathetic, his trying to flirt with her while staring at the women on stage. "That sounds divine." She slid closer to him, and he draped an arm around her shoulder, his fleshy fingers grazing the outside of her breast. Instead of punching him through the trachea — which severely tempted her — she sat there and laughed while they ate.

Juan Simone — another she was to eliminate — showed up as well and sat on the other side of her. Her eyes watered from the power of their cologne. How fortuitous. Two for the price of one made her life easier. They must have some other connection for them to sit together and not seem surprised to see each other here.

She could do it. Despite that, her heartbeat kicked up with more than just adrenaline. While the buzz it gave her reminded her why she'd loved her job, there was part that didn't jump on the bandwagon. That bit of her tensed, worried she'd be caught. She could spend the rest of her life in a Mexican prison. Never see Sean again. Her palms grew sweaty while nausea churned in her gut, and she had to bite the inside of her cheek to get her mind back in the game. Out or not for all those years, she had a job to do.

She muttered the information under her breath so they'd know two of her targets were with her. She'd intended to take them both out here, but hadn't planned on it being the same day or time.

She put her hand on each of their thighs and squeezed. "I really need to get going. But thank you"—she blinked and smiled at them both—"for such a wonderful time."

When Juan began to move, she held him still. "No need for you to get up. I'll climb over," she said silkily with a sexy grin.

His eyes lit up at the prospect, and she did, allowing her breasts to press against him as she delivered the concoction from her ring to Diego's inner thigh. On Juan, she scratched the back of his neck, apologizing with false sympathy when he said ouch.

Walking away with an extra swing in her hips, she murmured, "You have five minutes before they'll be out." With a wave for the doorman, she stepped into the sun and grunted as she ran into someone.

"DeSalvo," she hissed. The noise around them slowed until her entire world revolved around the man before her. Her heart rate, which had finally calmed down after the initial kick up, raced once more. However, this time, along with her fear over what he could do to her son, ran white-hot anger. How dare he take her baby from her? Could she just take him out here? Did she have enough poison left in the ring?

Forget the poison—she itched to reach her hands around his neck and squeeze the life from him. A buzzing in her ear snapped through the haze, which had begun to settle around her eyes as she'd sunk into the single-minded focus of killing DeSalvo.

"Let him go, Iggy. We need him alive to find Sean." Beckett's calm voice pushed her back into the world of control. "Detach."

Although he sounded modulated, she picked up on his own anger, and that helped her. He was with her on hurting the man. She flared her nose and inhaled deeply, taking in the scents of the city and the expensive cologne DeSalvo wore.

He stared at her from beneath the brim of his white fedora. "Busy, I see."

"Are you following me?"

"I wanted to watch you in action."

She smiled sweetly at him. "Give me a rifle, and I'll let you see it firsthand." Sugar might have dripped from her words, yet in no way did it disguise the venom.

"Such a violent woman."

He hadn't begun to see what she could do as a violent woman. "How's Sean?" She couldn't let him provoke her. She held onto Beckett's advice.

"I haven't seen him today."

"Anything happens to him, I'm coming after you." The words were low, the danger they promised vivid.

He took her arm. "Come with me."

She shook her head, making sure the ear with the bud stayed covered. "No, sorry."

He scowled at her. "Why not? Do you not recall I have your son?"

She thought about that every single second, bastard. "Because I have one more to kill today, and he's only in this place for a certain amount of time."

"So you killed someone in there?"

"No. I killed two. Why you're asking, I'm not sure. They won't be dead yet, the poison takes a bit of time, so tell whomever you have in there who was watching me it'll be about four minutes. I have some more." She stepped closer. "Would you like to see personally how it works?" The ring flashed in the sun.

DeSalvo took a step back, and she nearly gloated. "Don't even think about it. Something happens to me, and you never see your son again."

"I need to go. I'd really rather not be around when it's discovered they're dead." She slipped by him and flagged down a taxi. "He's got men in there," she said before slipping into the vehicle. "Be careful." The moment the words were out, she realized how rattled she was. Of course they knew he had men in there, they'd heard the entire exchange. She rubbed a hand down the side of her face. She had to get control. Her emotions were getting out of hand, and she was going to make a mistake.

Giving her next destination to the driver, she leaned back against the seat, then took the ring off and stored it in a pouch.

DeSalvo's unexpected appearance had considerably narrowed the window of opportunity to get them the antidote, but she had confidence her team would make it in time. She let go of any thoughts of those two scum.

Adrenaline continued to pump through her. And despite her misgivings about how that one went down, she'd forgotten how much she craved the burn the thrill brought her. This next one would be better.

A toy store appeared up the street on the right. "Can we stop here?" she asked the driver. "I'll be right back."

He parked and she jumped out, hurrying inside. Making her way back to where they sold children's walkie-talkies, she grabbed two packages and went to the counter to purchase them, along with the batteries required.

"You all right now?" the soft question rang in her ear.

Thanking the man at the register, she walked outside. "Fine." Once she was seated in the vehicle, the taxi got underway. She closed her eyes until he reached her destination. When she finally returned to the hotel, she'd owe Beckett some thanks for having her back, because she very easily could have blown the entire thing open and ruined it all.

Indigo paid the driver and roamed through the park, then found a bench to sit on. The area hadn't many people, and she opened her pack and got to work. She dismantled the radios and did some rewiring. From her bag, she withdrew a small recording device she'd set up earlier and set it on the bench. Casting occasional looks around, she finished her final preparations.

Taking the blood packs Beckett had filled, she put them in her pocket, then pulled out a small cassette player and listened to the recording, rewinding and playing it over and over until it was cued to the perfect spot. Then she attached it to one of the dismantled devices.

Using two strips of duct tape, she secured the speaker to the underside of the bench with the pretense of having dropped something to the ground through the back of the bench. After she'd ensured it wouldn't fall, she taped the items she'd continue to carry, not willing to risk that the walkie-talkie could fall and change the sound she needed to carry through the speaker.

When she got warm, she uncapped some water and drank, all the while keeping an eye out for her next target. He ran through this park every day and if he was on time—like usual—she had another ten minutes before he'd pass her.

"We got them back to where we're keeping them. Antidote's been delivered, and they're fine."

Lisa's statement, a welcome one. Indigo gazed around again, this time with more caution. The nearest person to her was an old man feeding the birds. He'd been there when she arrived, but she took another look at him.

If he was EGIS, it was a damn good disguise. She couldn't figure it out, but suddenly she felt as if she weren't alone.

· · ·

This habit Indigo Grey had of slipping away from the bullets that had her name etched on them annoyed her. At this rate, EGIS would get hold of her again, have her questioned, and perhaps learn the truth.

She checked her fingernail polish, frowning over the small chip in the left hand middle finger. With a practiced move, she opened her desk drawer and pulled out the pale pink hue and fixed the mistake. She replaced the bottle and blew on her nail.

She turned her attention from the computer screen depicting Indigo Grey walking away from a strip club, *somehow* avoiding her next assassin, to her black phone with its blinking light. A few more moments of waiting, then she paused the video feed and picked up the receiver.

"Why do I hear things like 'loose end' and 'unresolved' when it comes to Indigo Grey?" Anger coated the masculine voice.

"Why are you listening to things from other people?" She leaned back in her chair after switching it to speakerphone.

"Because I do not believe you are being fully truthful with me."

Unsure if it was a question or statement, she didn't answer. "I have contacted DeSalvo, informing him to keep the child until further notice. All attempts on her life are halted as of now. I want her after DeSalvo. They can fight each other. I have something else requiring my attention."

"What about me?"

She rose and smoothed her hands down her skirt. "I doubt you need me around for sex. I know of seven others alone who have shared your bed." She hung up, spun on her heels, and departed, laptop in hand. Brisk steps took her from the building to the waiting limo.

"Where to, Madam?"

She stared at her hands, inspecting flawless nails. "My plane."

"Very good, Madam."

Sliding along the leather seat, she waited for the door to close. Then she fixed herself a drink. As she sipped, a small smile crossed thin lips. This would work. All of it. Then all who'd doubted her would see. *He* would see.

Chapter Eight

The fact Iggy didn't seem to recognize him almost had Beckett smiling. Only years of experience kept it away. He could tell by her actions she was suspicious. He'd been in the park for hours feeding the damn birds and napping like old men did.

His body hadn't responded like an old man, by any means, when she came into view. She moved with such grace and sensuality it belied the point she had it in her to be a stone-cold assassin. A slight aura of innocence hovered around her. She sat there in pale pink shorts that drew his eye to her smooth and toned legs. Legs he loved having around his waist or over his shoulders.

Nope, not the time for those thoughts. He moved on. A white shirt—snug fitting—showcased her flat belly and full breasts.

God, he continued to have wet dreams about her breasts. Coughing, he tossed out more seed for the greedy birds. She rose from the bench, a frown on her face, only to bend over it for something on the other side.

He'd shame himself if this kept on.

A ragged sigh left him when she sat back down. Years. He'd managed without her for years. Now she was what he was most focused on. A little over a week. That was the time he had to survive being so close to her when he couldn't do anything about it.

Maybe not. Assuming she hadn't lied to him, they shared a son, one he was determined to learn about, one way or another. Which meant there'd be a lot more of Indigo Gray in his life. Because no matter what she said, he had every intention of being a father to Sean. Boys needed their fathers.

Another toss of birdseed, and he grunted when she got to her feet. She shouldered her bag, opened the book in her hand, and began walking away, her sleek ponytail swaying with each step. He made sure he didn't listen to his baser desires and turn to watch her walk out of sight.

Instead, he concentrated on something else. The feel of those silken strands flowing over his skin as he bunched his hands in her hair had his breathing shorten. The smoky look she shot him as he held her while he buried himself deep inside her.

Great! Now he was horny and sweaty.

"*Perdóneme.*" Excuse me.

Indigo's voice, smooth and apologetic, pulsed through him, courtesy of the earpiece he had. He didn't turn to see. That would be foolish and possibly ruin their work. If she used the same method as she'd previously done, the man had just a few minutes.

The third target appeared near the bench she'd been

seated at and was moving by it when gunshots rang out. Beckett ducked immediately, scanning for the shooter. The man she was to take out lay on his back, unmoving. Chaos erupted in the park, people screamed, some prayed, most ran.

Had she truly killed the man? And how had she pulled it off? He hadn't seen a weapon on her. They'd made up the blood packs, but she'd remained close lipped when he asked her how she was going to make it work since she didn't want to use poison this time.

Shoving up from the bench seat, he shuffled to the fallen man. "Indigo, where are you?" he muttered as he went.

No answer.

"Find her," he ordered.

At the body, Beckett checked for a pulse, but there was none. A hole in his chest continued to bleed. Christ, he never saw her shoot him. He had to be missing something. *Think.* She was as good as ever.

Indigo hadn't been by the man when he'd fallen, and this man had fallen backward. Had she been the one to shoot him, he would have fallen forward.

"We have this, sir." A voice spoke in Spanish.

Two cops crouched by him, and Beckett moved away to where another officer waited to ask him questions. He didn't argue, since Marco was one of the two by the body.

The interviewer, taking pity on his old bones, allowed him to sit on the bench. It was then he figured it all out. Brilliant, Indigo. Absolutely brilliant.

When he'd finally finished their question and answer, been given permission to leave, the item he'd seen sat securely in his pocket. All that remained of his disguise, when he made it to the room, was the reversible hat turned from tan into dark blue. It had taken him a while to get there, and he'd tried to get in touch with Indigo repeatedly as he walked. No luck.

"The reports all say fatal shooting." Marco said as he walked in the room.

"That's what we wanted, but he was alive when you deposited him with Lisa, right?"

"He's alive." Marco took a seat. "How'd Indigo pull that off?"

Beckett stepped forward and straddled a seat as he tossed the item from his pocket on the table.

Marco reached out and picked it up. "A speaker?" Marco chuckled. "She's good."

"Exactly." Beckett swelled with pride. She hadn't lost her touch; she was damn good.

"Explain," Lisa said over the speaker.

"She wired a walkie-talkie to work with just the one piece. She placed the speaker on the bench, nicked the target with poison, and timed the poison's effect with a broadcast of prerecorded gunshots. When we heard the mumbled words of her bumping into him, she'd planted a blood pack on him. Altogether, he appeared to have died in a random park shooting."

A grudging look of respect crossed Marco's face. "Where is she?"

Beckett shrugged. "No clue. I was in the park as the old man. Not quite up for running after young women."

"*She* is in her room."

They sat straighter when Indigo's voice came to them.

"You need to come down here." Beckett knew he was

demanding, but he wanted to see her.

"No. I'm going to sleep. Leave me alone."

It had been a hard couple of days for her. Him, too. Yet he wanted to see her for himself. Call it proprietary, or call it something else, it's what he wanted. He could survive without seeing her. They'd done so on all the ops they'd worked on together in the past, and he could do it now.

Marco looked him over and went on his way with a jerk of his head. He didn't argue and was soon lying in his bed, staring up at the ceiling, wishing beyond anything he had Indigo in his arms. Her body pressed against him, the scent of her in his nose as he breathed.

It wasn't meant to be.

• • •

Four days later, Indigo had disguised herself as a day laborer and followed the man to his job. She'd been chosen that day, too. How she'd managed to do it, he hadn't a clue. He'd watched her through a scope from a good distance away since there had been no way for him to be closer. She actually did the work, smoothing out the concrete poured for the foundation. Backbreaking, but she never slacked.

At the whistle, the laborers had gone out to the lunch truck. Her target, a father of three, got his sandwich and drink, then sat by himself. Indigo carried around the cooler with bottled water, handing out drinks to everyone. The target included. Other than a small smile, she never engaged him in conversation. Once that was done, she took herself back across the area to eat her own lunch.

Ten minutes later, the man had gone into cardiac arrest.

When the ambulance arrived, they confirmed the man had died. Honestly, he'd expected Indigo to leave, but she finished out the day and because of that, he stayed to cover her. Through the scope, he'd smiled as she slipped her day's wage into the pocket of another man while they climbed back into the truck that would return them to the pickup spot.

Lisa was taking their "confirmed kill" back to holding, and he'd gone to get something for Indigo to eat, only to come back to find her dead to the world on his bed. Beckett stared at the woman sleeping in his bed.

Each day she was away from her son, he could see a bit more humanity leave. He recognized the anger and the vengeance that burned in her. Was this how she saw him and how he was with EGIS? Sean was his son, as well. Would he be like this the more he accepted the role of fatherhood? How much did someone change when they had a child? Had they been together, a real couple—which would have been possible had she not gone dark—things might have turned out differently and Sean wouldn't have been kidnapped. Why did that disturb him so much? He clenched his jaw and took deep, calming breaths.

However, with her sleeping, he got the other Indigo. The one who brought out his protective instincts. The one who made him think back to that night in Louisiana and the ring that'd burned a hole in his pocket.

He shook off the thoughts. It wasn't going to be helpful to either one of them if her vanishing act pissed him off again. He sat beside her and froze.

The muzzle from her Glock pressed tight to his abdomen. "Easy, Iggy, it's me."

The semiautomatic slid back under her pillow. "What?"

He brushed some of her hair back from her face. She kept her eyes closed. "Nothing, go back to sleep."

"This is your and Lisa's room."

Was it wrong of him to imagine he heard some jealousy in her voice? Was it so wrong to hope he did?

"Yes."

"You share the bed?"

Okay, now he knew he heard some. Fighting back the grin, he shook his head. "Nope."

"Thought you were supposed to be a couple."

"We are. Outside of these doors. Not in here. On this side, we're colleagues."

"We were at one time as well. Didn't matter behind closed doors."

Settling his hand along the side of her face, he dragged his thumb along her full lips. "You, Indigo, I've always had a weakness for." His words had her opening her eyes and focusing her gaze upon him.

She shook her head and tried, unsuccessfully, to get free of his touch. "Don't."

"Don't what? Touch you like this? Like I know you enjoy? Or is that *don't* stop, as in 'keep touching me and do it more'?"

A tremble ran through her, and he leaned down to brush their lips together. He meant to keep it gentle. It would have worked, except she moaned into his mouth and melted into him. Passion exploded throughout his body, and he pressed her into the mattress.

Settling between her thighs, he rocked against her, showing her exactly what she did to him. How hard she made him. How much he wanted her. She widened her legs and cradled him more, hooking her legs around his waist.

Their tongues clashed in an angry battle for dominance. He wound his hands in her hair and tugged on the strands. God, the real thing put all wet dreams to shame. Her nails raked up his back, digging into his flesh and pulling a growl from deep in his throat.

He devoured her. Hungrily. As if it were his last chance and he'd never have the opportunity again to have her like this. Yes, he'd been with others since she left, but none of them could compare to her. Indigo ignited his blood just being in the same room. When they joined like this…combustible. Potently so.

It was too much and not enough. So long since he'd had her in his arms, he couldn't get enough. Deeper the kiss became. Longer it went on. Moreover, with each passing second he knew it would never be enough.

"Iggy," he uttered against her mouth.

He released one hand from her hair and cupped a breast, shoving under her shirt, seeking flesh and bra. Her bra was plain, nothing fancy, and it barely contained the pointed nipple that pushed determinedly into his palm. Her back arched, shoving her breast farther into his touch.

Nails found skin as she ripped his cotton tee up. Her touch, electric. Her moans, fire. His erection pressed hard against the fly of his jeans. Her hips undulated beneath him, mimicking the act they both so obviously craved. He couldn't hold out any more. His hand slipped down toward the waistband of her shorts. Dipping below, he cupped her mound. Her wetness was noticeable through the material.

Lifting the edge of her panties, which kept him from what he sought, he slipped his fingers under. So long, it had been so damn long. And it would be longer, because now wasn't the time. He needed more time with her. Not a stolen five minutes. He needed their issues resolved. He needed to meet his son. He had changed and wasn't a quickie-in-the-back-room-after-an-op kind of guy anymore.

He wouldn't be able to put it out of his mind until he sated his need for her, and it would take much longer than they had now. He reluctantly pushed away from her and put some much needed space between them. They calmed down and just sat there in silence, lost in their own thoughts. Although he'd bet they were on the same thing—Sean.

Lisa slipped in, her gaze taking it all in.

"I have some food coming up, so if you're staying, you need to hide, Indigo."

Indigo rose from the bed and hid her Glock. She never spoke, just walked to the door, peered out, then disappeared.

"Sorry." Lisa removed her sidearms.

"No reason to be." He willed his erection away.

She raked a hand through long blond hair as she ran her gaze over him. "I've already asked you this, but have you told her you love her yet?"

"Why should I say anything?" he asked.

She unhooked her pants and shoved them down her legs, which left her clad in workout attire. "So you can be part of your son's life."

"What?"

She went to the bathroom with clothes in hand, yet left the door open. Lisa reappeared in a loose silk top and flirty knee-length skirt. "You heard me fine, Beckett."

Talk paused while they accepted the room service delivery. He noticed she'd ordered enough for him as well. Lisa shut the door before moving to her bag and strapping a double duce gun to her right thigh. She followed that up with a stiletto to her left.

Beckett straddled a bench while she snagged some fries. It occurred to him that he'd just been in the room with a very attractive woman who'd stripped and redressed in front of him and had felt no arousal.

It took him a minute to realize Lisa had been talking to him. "I'm sorry, what did you say?"

She took a burger and fries then sat at the table. Her green eyes sparkled with amusement. "Didn't realize your wife was such a bore to you." All joviality left her features. "How are you?"

"Tired. Conflicted." Horny for Indigo. Frustrated and pissed his son was in some asshole's hands. Trying to figure out how to remain in Sean's life once this was over. He had to remain calm or he'd go off the deep end. If what he and Indigo were doing now didn't work, then all bets were off. He'd do things his way and fuck anyone who got in his way. He'd kill them all. Beckett swallowed, forcing himself to relax his hands from the fists they were in.

"I'd say take a nap, but I have a feeling that won't work."

She'd be correct. He left the bench and joined her at the table. Might as well eat something.

Lisa withdrew a file from her bag and dropped it before him. "In that case, let's try to figure out how Michael got the idea Indigo stole from him, and how we clear her name."

· · ·

"I've been thinking." Indigo propped her feet up on the dash as Beckett drove the next day.

"About?"

For the past hour, it had been silent in the Jeep. She observed him in her periphery. Ball cap low over his sunglasses, he rested one hand on the wheel while his right settled on his thigh.

"This entire thing"—she gestured with one hand—"the situation. Starting with first and foremost how the hell you knew I'd been arrested and where I was being kept."

He pursed his lips before peeking in her direction. "You mentioned that before."

"And I still don't have an answer from you." She straightened in the seat. "Which is why I am asking again."

"I can't tell you."

"Why not?" Her tone cold.

He gripped the wheel with enough force to turn his knuckles white. "Michael wouldn't tell me."

Beckett was beginning to question everything his life had been about the past many years. She wriggled her toes, wishing they'd already arrived at their next destination. She was getting stir-crazy. "So you must have a thought of your own on it."

"There's a mole. And someone's watching you."

So he'd arrived at the same conclusion. "I want to know who. And why. What makes you think there's a mole?"

He removed his hat briefly as he scratched his head. "We've been after DeSalvo for six years. He always manages to be one step ahead. It seems too much of a coincidence that he's the one who kidnapped our son."

She didn't like where this might be going. "Are you worried Lisa and Marco are it?"

"No." He flexed his hand and shrugged. "Then again, I never thought I'd be saying there was a mole in EGIS."

"Maybe…maybe you should go back and talk to Michael about your theory of a mole."

"I'm not leaving you." Those words were issued with such firmness she didn't dare argue.

"Just thinking of how you could resurrect your career. Save Lisa's and Marco's as well."

"I didn't ask them to help. They made their own decisions." He glared. "Stop trying to get rid of me."

"My father is looking into EGIS as well for ideas on who the mole may be."

Beckett grunted, and she rubbed the bridge of her nose. "How's your sister doing?"

Her question seemed to surprise him. She was trying to keep the mood lighter between them. He'd often spoken of his older sister, Evelyn, during their operations.

"Good. She's married now with two children. A girl, Phoebe, and a boy, Tucker. They live in Maine."

"How do you like being an uncle?"

"I don't get to see them much. I send things, but you know how it is—we don't get much time off and when we do, there's always the fear that we'll bring danger if we hang out a lot with them."

She understood that perfectly. "I'm sure they appreciate what time you give them."

"Family is important." His gaze hit her direct, and she knew he meant them as well.

• • •

Indigo leaned against the sink of the tiny motel they'd stopped at. Beckett had paid cash and she'd stayed out of sight until he'd returned with the key. They'd gotten pizza to go, then she took a shower. Now she hesitated going back out to the room.

He was such a presence. After working with him for so long, she'd learned to do the job when it came time, ignoring the extent to which she'd fallen for the man. Now it was like starting over. Every second she spent with him had her gravitating to him more. And more. So much it was becoming a distraction.

"Get a hold of yourself, Indigo," she muttered.

Chewing on her nail, she took several deep breaths before opening the door and stepping out. Beckett sat on the single queen bed—he swore they didn't have any doubles available—flicking through the channels on the television. He turned his head and her entire body responded as if he'd touched her. Goose bumps popped up, and she hid the shiver best she could.

"Anything?" she asked, gesturing to the television with her head.

"Not a peep. Michael's keeping a lid on our escape. If he did send our likeness to authorities, they didn't put it out on the newswires."

"Good." She went to the chair at the desk, where she had everything of theirs charging, and sat. "Do you have a copy of the file you said Lisa had compiled?"

"Yes." He swung off the bed and went to their bags. Her gaze lingered on the firm ass he had, amplified by the jeans he wore. Every motion fluid, each action dangerously arousing. She shook her head and tried to focus. Riffling through one, he pulled out a folder.

"Here."

Walking to her, he handed it over but wouldn't release it. She lifted her eyebrow in silent question. Without a word, he allowed her to take it.

"I'm going to get ice," he said. Then he was gone.

She sighed. "How am I going to do this? All I can think about is jumping him."

Carrying the file, she went to the bed, sat where Beckett had been, and started to read. Some of the names weren't new to her. She needed the computer her father had given her to do some checking.

She wasn't sure when she dozed off, but when she woke she lay entwined in bed with a familiar body. How he'd come back in the room and done that without her knowledge, she hadn't any clue. Then again, this was Beckett, and she trusted him to keep her safe. And the exhaustion weighing on her probably played a large part; she couldn't say which singular item it was. Perhaps it was a mix of them all.

One of her legs was wedged between his powerful ones. His arms circled her completely, holding her tight to his chest. Her hands lay plastered against his back—his bare back—and warm skin. Her head rested over the steady beating of his heart. A blanket covered them, and she wondered briefly if he was naked. With her wearing jeans, she couldn't tell.

She shifted her weight, and his hold loosened a fraction until she settled, then it tightened again. It had been so long since she'd slept like this. Why not take advantage?

"You think too loud." Beckett's chest rumbled as he spoke. "Go back to sleep, Iggy. Just sleep."

His breath was warm on her ear, and it sent more shivers

down her spine. Licking her lips, she nuzzled closer to his chest and did as he ordered. Went back to sleep. It was nice having someone near she trusted. Only with him was she able to completely let her guard down and sleep.

They remained tangled in bed when she woke again. This time, however, she lay on top of him, her hands at his crotch, and she knew he wore boxers. Nothing else. Her fingers flexed instinctively when they smoothed over his cock. Immediately it hardened, and his hips bucked.

Her body grew slick. She knew what pursuing this venue would turn into. Pleasure. Raw. Primal. Exquisite. She clenched him again and groaned when his hands moved from her back to cup her butt.

"God, Iggy," he moaned.

Lifting her head, she sought his mouth, desperate for the connection she'd not had since she'd left him. His lips were warm and firm, opening at her slight pressure. His tongue waited for hers, and they lightly stroked along each other, heat building. It wasn't rushed—this was more exploratory. Relearning.

She moved her hands up so she could sink them into his thick hair. It was softer than she recalled. Digging her fingers into the strands, she tugged and nipped at his lower lip. Her eyes opened, and she found herself lost in his deep blue gaze. The exhaustion in his gaze faded by the moment as desire increased.

Almost too personal and not what she was ready for, so she closed hers again. Focusing on the kiss, she increased the depth. Her tongue surged through his mouth, stroking the sides and roof before coaxing it to follow her back where she drew on it until deep-throated groans emerged as his pelvis flexed against her. His fingers dug into her butt as he set a rhythm against her that had her panting into his mouth.

"Beckett!"

His answer was to roll them over so she was on the bottom. Widening her legs so he could settle there, she cradled him as the kiss went on, his hips continued to piston, and her breath eluded her.

"I want you, Iggy."

There were so many things wrong with this. Numerous reasons why it shouldn't be allowed to continue any further. She knew it. Knew he knew it. Just like she knew neither of them gave a damn. Right here, right now, it was all about one thing. Them.

Her answer was to slide her hand in his boxers and curl her fingers around his rigid length. It pulsed in her hand, and she whimpered. Beckett climbed off her and had her naked in seconds. He palmed a breast and sucked her nipple in his mouth.

She gasped, hand threading into his hair and pressing him tight to her. He moved until she writhed on the sheets. A purr escaped as he nudged his thickness inside her.

Her eyelids fluttered at the joy of having him inside her again. It had been so long. So damn long. She moved her hands to his shoulders and dug her nails into his bare skin. His skin slick with sweat as he thrust into her.

"Damn, I've missed you, Iggy," he moaned in her ear. "Missed this."

Words escaped her, and she undulated against him, needing more. Needing everything he'd give her. It might have been years since they were together in such an intimate way, but they made love as if it hadn't been but a few hours. They had always been good together, and it seemed as though the time apart hadn't mattered.

Her body met his thrusts with ease, her legs elevated around his waist, drawing him in deeper, allowing the high he gave her to take over her body, escorting her to the plane of ultimate pleasure. She came hard as he continued to drive home inside her, internal muscles clenching around him. He stiffened and growled as he shot his release deep within her.

Spent and sweating, she slid her arms around his shoulders and drew him down upon her. She wanted him as close as she could have him. He buried his face in the side of her neck and pressed kisses there.

"Iggy."

"Hmm?"

She was so comfortable all she wanted to do was close her eyes and drift off into the land of dreams. He pushed up and put them nose to nose. Lost in his gaze, she waited for him to say something. He didn't. Silence reigned as he watched her intently. Almost like he was memorizing how she was at this exact moment.

He began thickening inside her, and she shifted beneath him. Beckett took her hands and laced their fingers before positioning them above her head, stretching her out.

"We're not done." He dipped his head and nipped her lip. "Not even close."

Sleep was overrated. Placing the soles of her feet on the mattress, she bucked against him. "My pace, Iggy. Nice and slow until you're burning."

She licked her lips. "Beckett."

He began moving again. Slow strokes. Instantly her body responded, and she found herself moving in tandem with him again. In and out. Slow and agonizingly tempting thrusts.

"Stop trying to find a way to get me to go faster, Iggy. I want slow. I want to feel you tighten around me, watch your eyes as you come around my cock. Kiss your lips and hear your breathy little moans as they turn to screams of passion while I fuck you. Hard and soft. See how much you can take before you beg me to let you come again."

Her insides trembled. She was ready to beg now. Her words wouldn't fall from her mouth, her throat was too dry. He continued to move within her with those slow measured strokes destined to drive her insane.

She tried to move, but he had her pinned. "No, baby. I like you like this, spread out beneath me." His eyelids lowered, but she knew he focused on her breasts. She closed her eyes and tried to break the growing emotional connection between them. This needed to be strictly about mutual pleasure. Not futures, pasts, or anything else.

Over and over, Beckett took her to the edge only to bring her back. Until she panted and cried out for release, then he let her find it. When they finally collapsed from exhaustion, she found herself tucked tight to his hard body. Limbs entwined. As she drifted into slumber, his deep voice whispered, sounding almost as if she imagined it.

"Mine, Iggy, mine."

If only it were true.

She woke before Beckett and slowly untangled from his embrace, then headed for the shower and stood under the hot, pounding spray. *Great job, Indigo Grey, sleep with the man, no protection, multiple times.* She'd already seen what could happen when she did that. The man was potent as all get-out, because she'd only slept with him once without protection and had ended up pregnant. What exactly did she think was going to happen doing it all night long?

She was on the Depo shot. Squeezing her eyes shut, she counted back to when she'd had it last. With everything going on, she'd forgotten about that. She was due for another, but maybe she was covered; perhaps it hadn't been long enough for the chemical to get out of her system.

She groaned. Not something she needed to focus on right now. Finishing DeSalvo's list and clearing her name was top priority, so she and Sean could live their life without her worrying Michael would show up and ruin it.

She showered and dried off, then reached for the pile of clothing she'd brought in with her. Securing the thin steel between her shoulder blades, she looked up when the door opened and Beckett walked through. Heat hit her immediately. Why couldn't she think straight around him? Not good. She had to get her head on straight.

"I'll be done in a minute."

Shoving home the last of the blades, she gathered her hair and pulled it into a high ponytail. The entire time, Beckett leaned against the doorframe, watching her. He wore nothing but his boxers, and she had the hardest time not allowing herself a stray glance.

"All yours," she said, brushing by him.

She made it one step by him before he captured her upper arm, halting her. "We don't have time to waste, Beckett. I'll be ready and have the Jeep packed by the time you're done."

"So that's how it's going to be?" He shook his head, disgust on his face. "Fine." Beckett released her and slammed the door behind him.

She exhaled and almost followed him in there but at the last second continued on her original plans. Indigo stood at the back of the vehicle, tossing the final bag in on the flattened backseat when he strode from the motel room.

"To damn hot for my own peace of mind." He'd dressed in tight black jeans, boots the same color, and a dark blue shirt, which highlighted those impressive muscles in his upper body. "Too damn hot!" Focusing on what she had to do, she ensured nothing was loose and stepped free.

"Let's go." His words were brusque, and she swallowed her response.

Hopping in, she shut the door behind her, and thought about removing the doors. When Beckett settled beside her, she started the engine. With a brief stop for him to turn in the keys, she set up the GPS for their next destination. The town wasn't that far away, and she'd be able to take care of another on the list.

Once the Jeep pulled out he asked, "What did you pull from Lisa's files?"

"I ran down some of the things, got some names. The closest one now lives in the Ozarks. I'll head there and see what they know after I finish this."

"How'd you find him? Or her?"

They headed down the road, morning air flowing over them. "I checked their aliases and did searches with different versions of them until I landed on one that looked like it fit."

"You got access to EGIS's files?"

Why did he sound surprised by that? "I still have the ones from when I worked for EGIS. Off-site storage so I could always get to it if needed." A light shrug. "Didn't think it would be needed, though. More like hoped I wouldn't need them."

He reached for the computer lying between them and flipped the lid. She didn't speak while he powered it up and pulled up the files she'd been comparing.

"A few of these are dead now. I'll make notes."

She watched him in her periphery. Stoic. Unemotional. Businesslike. The Beckett she'd worked with so many days and nights over years past. Nothing like the lover she took to her bed. Nevertheless, it helped, because she needed his distance to remain focused. It would be harder at the end if she allowed herself to get emotionally involved with him. Again. No matter that he'd started questioning Michael's actions, Beckett was an agent. Would always be. He'd find a way to keep his job at EGIS, which meant every time he came for a visit, and she knew he would, he'd put Sean's life in danger. She needed distance from this man for her sake. For Sean's safety.

Chapter Nine

Indigo wiped the sweat from her brow and kept going. Her harsh breathing the only sound in the room. One a.m. had passed thirty-seven minutes ago—if she were watching, of course. She should be sleeping, but every time she closed her eyes all she could see and hear was fear and sorrow from her son. The only time that left her alone was the shared moments with Beckett at night. Something she couldn't do again—his touch muddled her thoughts and destroyed the edge she needed to fulfill this mission. It would be far too easy to let him take over and solve it for her. It wasn't his problem to resolve. The ones who messed with her life were for her to handle. All which brought her thoughts back to Sean.

It burned through her. The need to hold her child again. Smell the shampoo in his hair. Feel his arms around her. The cry burst out of her, and she crumpled to the floor, her arms no longer able to continue supporting her. Luckily, she was only doing push-ups.

Deep soul-wrenching sobs tore from her as she tried to contain them. *Don't break down now. One more day.* One day closer to finishing all this crap so she could get Sean and take him back home.

Slapping her hand over her mouth—as if that would stop the cries—she closed her eyes. It wasn't working. She pressed her fingertips over her eyes and tried to breathe slower. She had no clue where her son was, just had to go on faith that DeSalvo meant what he said and that Sean was fine.

One day. She had one day to take out this target before he left the country. It was as if he knew he carried a bull's-eye on his forehead. Plans changed after he made them, extra security. Hell, it was as if he'd been forewarned. Nothing that made her job easier—not for actually keeping him alive. Were she actually killing him, it would have been done by now.

As she pushed to her feet, the cell phone she'd been ordered to keep on her at all times rang. Her heart skipped a few beats and instantly, a sheen of sweat broke out over her skin. Reaching for it, she ignored the not-so-slight tremble in her hand.

"Yes?"

"Not asleep? I thought it might ring a few more times."

"What do you want?" She sat on the bed's edge. If only she knew where DeSalvo was, she'd go after her son and to hell with anything else.

"There's been a change in one of your targets."

Iron infused her spine, snapping her upright. She'd been concerned something like this would happen.

"No comment?"

Yeah, he enjoyed her misery. Got off on it.

"Who's the new target?" She sat back on the bed regardless of how her body sang with energy.

"Such a good girl. So willing to go along with me."

Oh, it was so easy to imagine his throat in her hands as she squeezed, slowly, and watched the life leak out of him. "You have my son. Quit screwing around and tell me what you want."

He tsked, and she fought for control. "I wanted to believe you were working alone. To believe you'd listened to my orders. However, I have…never mind. This is not important to you. New target. Jorge Fuentes."

She frowned as that name tickled her memory banks. Where had she seen or heard it? Also, what the hell was he talking about, believing she wasn't working alone? Lord help any EGIS agent who'd been seen following her and jeopardized her son's safety.

She wasn't sure how he'd done it, but Marco had pulled in a few more agents to help. From what she'd gathered, since she didn't interact with them, they assumed they were here under Michael's orders.

"You want me to kill Jorge Fuentes?"

"Yes, and you have a little longer time to accomplish this in. I suggest you waste none of it and get it done. I will be sending you something soon I am sure you want to see."

She expected nothing less from the weasely bastard. Deep breath to relax, and she nodded. An uneasy feeling churned in her gut. "It will be done."

The moment she had control of her emotions, she picked up the phone her father had given her and called him. She swiped a pencil and pad of paper as well.

"What?" he answered on the first ring.

"I need to know all you can find about a man named Jorge Fuentes, including location. And if you can trace the last number that just came to my phone."

"Hang on."

Beckett returned to the room while she waited. She filled him in, and he handed her a file. "From Marco," he said.

She flipped it open as her father got back on the line.

"This is what I have on him. Jorge Fuentes is one of the good guys. He spearheaded one of the causes not to harbor drug runners, terrorists, or anyone who'd bring shame to Mexico." Her father's tone was brisk and businesslike.

No wonder DeSalvo wanted him gone. Many supporters of Fuentes's ideals and beliefs had given birth to cries for him to run for the presidency. DeSalvo wouldn't want a man whom he couldn't buy off that high in power.

"Anything else?" she asked.

"Not on him, other than Fuentes is in the United States right now."

She jerked her head up, Beckett watching her. "He's in the States?"

"Yes. Right now he's out in California and has a few more appearances scheduled. The last one is Arkansas."

"Arkansas?" She pointed her pencil at Beckett. "This isn't making sense." She inhaled deeply. "What about the number?"

"Also in the U.S."

"So Sean is being held in the States?" Hope bloomed in her chest.

"That's where this number originated from."

"Where in the U.S.?"

"Wyoming."

Her heart thudded. She dropped the pencil and closed her eyes. "Where?"

"Cheyenne."

"I have to go. Thank you and sorry for—"

"Stop thanking me for helping you get my grandson back." He hung up.

"The States?" Beckett crouched before her, placing his hands on her thighs. "Sean's in the U.S.?"

"DeSalvo's phone is there, at least. In Wyoming."

He shook his head. "Why is Wyoming such a shock?"

"We live there." She clamped her lips shut the moment she said the words.

His expression told her he'd already filed it away.

She cleared her throat. "DeSalvo called and changed a target. He wants me to take out Jorge Fuentes, and the man just happens to be in the States touring."

"Will he give you longer?"

"Yes, but he warned me to hurry it up. Also said there'd be something I'd want to learn that he'd be sharing soon." She rubbed her temples. "I need food." She also needed to be alone and think. She pushed by him and out the door to head to the nearby convenience store.

• • •

Beckett balled his fists as the door latched behind Indigo after she stomped out. A completely different woman at night in his arms than now, during the day. He'd not backed off and given her space at night. He wanted her off her game when it came to him. So he pressed. Held her. Fucked her. Made love to her.

Each time for him the lines became more and more blurred, the waters more muddied. He'd gotten in so deep he was nearly to the point of not caring if he ever got out again.

He didn't want to think what she'd been doing in here while he helped Marco drag a body to the vehicle for transport.

He knew what the old Indigo preferred to do after a mission—have sex. She worked off her excess energy that way. This Indigo he didn't recognize. Not that he'd be averse to sex with her again.

But she continued to withdraw. The amount of strain she had on her slender shoulders had started to crack the shell she'd erected around her. Prior missions, they'd always kept up a light banter. Now she barely spoke. She was all about the business and getting it finished. The last "assassination" hadn't gone as planned, and the next thing he knew, she was walking up to the guy and stabbing him.

"What are you doing?" he'd demanded afterward.

"The placement of the wound looks mortal. Get down here and have Marco or Lisa treat him when they get him stashed. He'll live." She'd given a cold response and moved on, blending into the crowd with ease. The day following that one she'd barely said more than ten words to him. She cried at night and just rolled inside herself.

Worrying about Sean and doing DeSalvo's dirty work, then hiding in a cheap motel room to ferret out who'd set her up at EGIS and discover a way to clear her name had just about kicked her ass. His, too.

He opened the computer her father had sent with them

and pulled up a map of Wyoming. He hadn't any clue what the man had done to get internet access on this thing, but he was grateful for his skills.

His thoughts drifted to the life Indigo had built with their son. How was she as a mother? She'd said she was part of the PTA and baked cookies. The Iggy he remembered didn't cook; they'd always eaten out. The mother side was one he wanted desperately to learn more about.

What part of the state did she live in? How would he fit in? He wouldn't let her keep Sean from him—he *would* be part of his life. No matter what happened, Sean was his son as well.

That brought back the issue about EGIS and what his future with them held. At the time he'd acted, helping her get away from EGIS to save their son had been his only concern, but lately, he'd been contemplating what that meant for his future with them.

Did it really matter if it came to EGIS versus his family? The place that had given him a home and a family versus Indigo and Sean.

She'd left because she was pregnant, so why was his decision to leave, if it came to it—and according to Iggy it was—such a hard one for him to make?

While he was furious about EGIS's willingness to sacrifice Sean by locking Iggy up, he understood how the agency did things. Hell, Michael might not want him back after his disobeying orders. In spite of it all, the man had his loyalty for what he'd done for him all those years ago, and for that reason he'd give the director the benefit of doubt. Helping him find his way out of the darkness. Giving him the opportunity to reunite with his sister and be part of her life.

He hated that these thoughts had begun to haunt him; he needed to be focused on the stakes 100 percent and not worried about what might or might not happen. He could always get another job, so if Michael didn't want him back, he'd survive.

Beckett stretched as Indigo strode back in the room. Conversation had been at a minimum today while they cruised down to this hotel. He'd spent a great deal of time on the computer; she'd purchased the supplies so the GPS could be plugged in simultaneously. Indigo must have gotten up early to peruse the files from Lisa, because she hadn't touched them while he'd been awake.

He focused on the woman walking across the carpeted floor toward him. Each stride fluid and sensual without even trying, a naturally seductive woman. Her loose T-shirt was beige and had a black tiger silkscreened on the front. She had her knives on her, and knowing her, a firearm as well.

Olive-green cargo pants rode low on her hips, exposing a bit of her stomach as she approached. Each flash of her smooth skin had his blood pressure rising. What was he thinking? Just because he'd fucked her last night, everything would revert back to how it had been before?

Okay, so perhaps he had. Sue him, he was a red-blooded male who had deep feelings for this woman. *His* woman. Apparently, his body—heart, mostly—didn't give a rat's ass that she'd left him or kept knowledge of his son from him. His thoughts were something else, and it still pissed him off.

He wanted to see her with Sean. Be able to see the re-laxed look on her expression. See her happy. Hear his son call him Dad, or whatever he wanted to use. Learn what it was like to be a father in more than name only.

"What now?" he asked.

She rested her hip against the dresser and stared at the chips in her hand. "I need to double-check some information I found in some of the files." She offered him a soft drink, keeping the water for herself.

Grabbing the bottle, he uncapped the Mountain Dew and drank. Indigo hated the stuff. Personally, he could—and had—lived on it.

The bed dipped as she lowered herself to the mattress, and she took the computer from his lap. He didn't try to hide the fact he'd been looking up Wyoming.

Her head remained down, focused on the screen. She was frustrated. Computers weren't her foray. She preferred to fight head-on, not spend time researching and compiling information.

Thankfully, her father had done a lot of legwork for her. She hadn't fully trusted Marco and had depended on her old man to do it instead. So, as far as Lisa and Marco knew, they were strictly going after DeSalvo and Sean. They didn't know about the possibility of a mole.

"I'm looking at some people who I think I need to talk to. This is the second time Arkansas has been mentioned, and we both know how I feel about coincidences."

He was with her on that. Grateful she hadn't shut him out, he listened while he drank. "After we get to him, who-ever *he* is, you have any idea what we'd do?"

"I need to ask him some questions about one of the guys in his old group."

Beckett opened her container and withdrew some fries to give her. She ate them. "So you have an idea who it was that stole this stuff?"

"Two hunches."

He waited a few moments and frowned when she didn't say anything else. "And they would be?"

She gestured to the screen. "Do you remember Richard Chisom?"

The image was familiar. A fit man with dark brown hair and green eyes, ones that held a calculated gleam, as if while having his picture taken, he was plotting. "Didn't know him well, but I remember him. Why do you think it's him? I heard he died a few years back."

"He had access to all codes and could go anywhere in the building. I'm not so sure he's truly dead like it says. Duke Randolf, who we're going to find and talk to once we reach the States, knew him best, and I just need to be confident things are what they seem. If I can time the Jorge Fuentes thing for when he's in Arkansas, then I can haul ass up to this man's place after." She shut the lid on the computer, stretched out her legs, and drank some water while she ate. "The other is someone who's still at EGIS. If that's the case, we need to start looking at the secretaries and other staff."

"Even Michael's secretary?" He shook his head, unable to remotely picture the older woman doing such a thing. "No way."

"Why not? Short of Michael, she has the most access. Secretaries are typically overlooked by their bosses. They're entrusted with codes and access. Why not Julie? She's the second most powerful person at EGIS, even if no one wants to verbalize it. She's run every aspect of his life at EGIS since it got off the ground. She was there before he recruited me."

He nodded. "Me, too." He just couldn't wrap his head around it. "But Julie? She's a—"

She cocked a brow at him. "You of all people should accept that doesn't mean a damn thing. I'm sure he vetted her like he did all of us before hiring, but how up on her is he staying? She's become such a pillar in his life. It wouldn't be the first time someone became lax with a person they're overly familiar with. Not saying it's her, but that it might be one of the secretaries at EGIS. Someone who's been there awhile, at least before I left, since my code was used."

"I just find it hard to picture Julie wheeling out AKs, ARs, RPGs, and explosives."

"Secretaries have bills to pay, too. Also, habits that might not be so easily broken. And to be fair, I can't picture myself wheeling out all that stuff, either."

He grunted. She had a point there. "Fine, so we check them along with any of the janitorial staff. They also have access pretty much anywhere and tend to blend. What's the deal with you and your father?"

Indigo ate the fries in her hand. "What deal?"

"You two seem at odds."

A harsh chuckle escaped from her. "You and I are at odds, Beckett. The old man and I are...have an extremely tenuous relationship."

"Why?"

"Looking to psychoanalyze me? Don't. We all have people with whom we don't see eye to eye. He'll do what it takes to help me get Sean back, and that's really all I care about. Whatever his distaste for me and for what I did won't affect that."

"I had no doubt about that, Iggy. I'm just curious."

She rubbed the bridge of her nose. "Can we drop it? I'd rather not go into family history right now."

"Family is important." He gave her a pointed look.

As he sat there with the only woman he'd ever loved, he realized more and more just how true his statement was. He just had to be willing to fight for the one he wanted. Including when it came to EGIS and his future there. Or not. She nodded, wiped her mouth, and shoved her napkin inside the Styrofoam container, then climbed off the bed and tossed it in the trash.

When she returned to the mattress, the computer was back in her hand. Indigo sat cross-legged on the paisley bedspread and began typing at a furious speed.

"What are you doing?" He opened the other container to find a piece of cake and scooted a bit nearer to her.

"Trying to find out more about Richard."

"I thought you already had it all."

"Not sure if there is or not. I downloaded everything my father sent and what I pulled from the files. Not to mention I'm a bit leery to be online so much."

"You think Michael has someone on it? Or are you thinking Marco is following what we're doing."

"Most definitely Michael has someone looking for any trace of me. I don't think it's Marco, but I'm not convinced the man hasn't been reporting back to Michael. My father made it secure but, sue me, I'm leery."

"Another reason you have the electrical tape over the camera?"

"Hell, yes. If they get access to this I don't need them tapping in whenever they want."

"Open your mouth."

She didn't hesitate, just did as he said, and he slid in a piece of the layered pound cake he'd gotten for dessert.

She'd enjoy it, as it was filled with raspberry jam and lemon curd, complete with buttercream frosting.

He couldn't close his eyes and save himself from the look of pure bliss that spread across her face. A purr of pleasure slipped from her mouth. His pants tightened when her tongue sneaked out and licked her lips, searching for the last bit of taste.

"What if this Duke refuses to talk?"

He ate a bite himself; it was delicious, but he'd be content watching this woman on the bed with him eating it all. When she allowed them to shine through, her expressions were so real, tangible, and honest.

"He'll talk to me."

There was no disguising her meaning. She'd get what she wanted one way or another. He watched her work in silence and ate his cake slice, occasionally holding up a bite for her. She was changing again, right before his eyes. The desperation and fear she'd portrayed when he picked her up in Mexico had vanished, only to be replaced with the focused calm he'd so admired about her during their missions. Her cracks were refilling because she tasted victory in their future. It was honing her focus.

After feeding her the last bite, he set the container aside and rested on his side, head propped up on one hand. The grip of her Glock stuck out from the back of her cargo pants and he knew she had knives on her back. Not to mention one strapped to her leg *under* the clothing she wore. Left leg, upper thigh. Hot as sin to have her wearing it while he took her, hard and fast.

Don't go there. He tried cautioning himself, but it was fruitless. How could he not? She was right there; all he would have to do was reach out his arm, and he could touch her. Glide his hand along her silken skin. Push up the short shirt she wore, exposing more of her flat belly. Lean in and allow his lips to follow that same trail up her body until nothing else mattered.

Chapter Ten

Indigo found it hard to concentrate. Beckett's focused stare had her heart thudding. Every synapse in her body was on alert, and she wanted nothing more than to sway toward him. She had no reason to continue staring at the screen before her. The information hadn't changed since she'd read it in the Jeep, but she used it as a buffer to keep from doing what she'd wanted to do since she woke up this morning.

Her body knew she wasn't focusing on the task ahead of them for tomorrow and it unceasingly reminded her of tall, dark, and handsome stretched out beside her. In her periphery, she could make him out. Jean-encased legs, black boots hanging off the mattress, and a worn shirt with "Poison" scrawled across the front. Although she couldn't see his face, she knew he wore his hat. Beckett loved to wear ball caps. Hat or no, his gaze homed in on her.

Eyes glued to the screen before her, she moved her finger, scanning through the information she'd compiled about Richard Chisom. The words flashed by and nothing new stuck. She couldn't learn any more about him.

"I'm not going to go away. You can't just pretend I'm not here."

"What makes you say that?" She struggled to ignore how much she loved his smooth voice floating over her.

"The way you're staring at the screen without seeing what's scrolling by." He shifted closer. "Years might have passed, Iggy, but you're still you, I'm me, and no one knows your body better than I do."

"Sure about that?" she snipped. He was right, although she'd never admit it—no one knew her better than he did.

"Yes." Absolute confidence poured from him with that one simple word.

"How can you? You don't know what I've done the past eight years. Or who, as the case may be."

He pressed the lid of the laptop until it clicked shut. She kept her attention riveted to the black surface as he walked that same hand up her arm, her shoulder, to touch her chin, then guide her head to the left so their gazes met. Would it be wrong to jump into the depths of his eyes and drown, never wishing to come up for air?

"Because of you, and what you did."

"What did I do?" How the heck was she supposed to think about what needed to be done when every last one of her senses were concentrated on him?

"You named our son Sean." His thumb traced her lower lip, upper, then lower one more time. "You named him after my grandfather." He inched closer. "It took me a while to re-alize that, but I've had a lot of time to think while we've been driving. I went over our conversations and remembered the one where I told you about Grandpa Sean and how much he meant to me growing up."

She had to keep a distance from him. Somehow. Best way she knew was to pick a fight with him. Did she want to? No. She *wanted* to turn her face to his hand. Kiss the palm, move closer, and trail her lips over him. Again. Just allow herself the indulgence of being in his arms once more.

"Coincidence, I'm sure. You were very clear on not wanting children. Why would I name my child after someone who meant something to you?" She pulled away from his touch, ignoring her body's protest.

Beckett barely blinked, just watched her with steadfastness. "Doesn't matter what you spout, Indigo. I know the truth." He wouldn't rise to the bait. Not this time.

"Really? How do you know I'm not lying about Sean being your son just to get your help?"

The look on his face told her he'd already considered that. Probably more than once. It struck deep as she realized he had every right to wonder. She watched the myriad of emotions on his features. He didn't want to argue with her. The compassion in him tempted her to cave and let him be the strong one for a while. She couldn't. This was *her* mess to get out from under.

"You're trying to make me mad, Iggy. It's not going to work."

She lifted a shoulder indolently. "All part of my grand plan."

He readjusted his hat, some of his thick hair falling forward over his face. She itched to touch him, brush it back so she had a clear and unimpeded view of his intense eyes. "You named *our* son after my grandfather. Very telling in my book."

"Can we stop with the nicety crap, Beckett?"

"Why are you so set on fighting with me?" He got off the bed, moving toward her with purposeful determination. "Is it because that's the only time you don't have to face your feelings? The regret you have over leaving like you did? Not telling me about my son?"

She backed until the edge of the low desk stopped her. Bracing her hands on the top, she clenched the edge, wishing things had been different.

"I don't run from my feelings, Beckett. I leave that to the experts." She raised an eyebrow and gave him a pointed look.

"I didn't run from my feelings for you, Indigo."

"Not how I remember it. You continually told me it was just fun between us. Nothing serious, despite being exclusive with each another. Didn't want to get tied down, no *kids*, no commitment. We'd been getting too serious for you—you thought it might be best to slow down even more." She winced over the bit of whine in her tone.

A tic appeared in his jaw. "I recall that. You do realize people can change, right?" He jammed his cap down on his head.

"Of course they *can*. The real question is if they do."

He stopped right before her, his large body looming over her. His gaze on hers, his hat on his head. Everything about him screamed *warrior*—his movements, his poise, and the way he noticed everything around him.

"I want to be part of his life."

"No."

And lest she forget the raw power he exuded and

his determination, it flashed across him in the space of a heartbeat. He gave a slight shake of his head as if having a hard time accepting what she'd just voiced. "I'm sorry, did you just tell me I can't be part of my son's life?"

If anyone happened to be listening to their conversation, they would have made the assumption it was an amicable one. She, however, knew better. No tone, no inflection of any sort—the words flowed from him as if he'd not a care in the world. But Beckett Hanson was livid. Apparently, she didn't respond swiftly enough, because he stepped farther forward, one of his powerful legs wedging between hers. He lowered his head, and she shivered, courtesy of his addictive scent.

"Is that what you're saying, Indigo?"

The anger rolled off him in thick, dominant waves. He stood before her, coiled like a panther, ready to strike. Yet at the same time, his expression was completely composed.

"Is it?"

She swallowed. "Yes."

A rough chuckle escaped him, one that held no humor at all. "You wanted me angry enough to not focus on wanting to fuck you into exhaustion. Congrats, you've got it. I'm pissed. Do you care to tell me why I'm not going to be allowed in my son's life?"

"You're EGIS."

He didn't blink, just stared at her, flames raging unchecked in his eyes. His thick lashes lowered slightly. "Your point being, what, exactly?"

"I don't want my son growing up in this life. I left EGIS to keep him safe. Keep the ugliness of this shit from touching him."

He arched an eyebrow and gave her a stare identical to

the one she'd recently given him. "How's that been working out for you?"

Ouch. Low blow. Okay, she deserved that. She glanced away from him. "Not well, thank you. But if you think I'm going to let him be close to you while you're remaining in this line of work, you're sorely mistaken."

"He's my son."

"I'm his mother. EGIS is poison, and you damn well know it. We make enemies all over the world. I'm not risking my son's life anymore. It's bad enough I have to deal with my past in keeping him safe. Adding yours as well? Hell no."

He gripped her chin and forced an eye connection. "I wasn't asking for your permission, Indigo. I was telling you I want to be part of his life."

She bristled. "You can tell me whatever you want. Don't necessarily mean it'll happen."

The hold on her chin tightened. "You'd keep him from me?"

"You're a threat to him as long as you're with EGIS. I can't tell you that you have to quit working there or doing that kind of job."

"Damn straight."

"But...*but* I am Sean's mother, and I will keep what I feel to be danger away from him."

"Don't make me fight you on this."

"Fight how? You're not on the birth certificate. For all intents and purposes, he's mine."

Beckett leaned close, the tips of their noses touching. "Don't go down this road, Iggy. You really don't want to back me into a corner. Sean is my son, and I have the right to be in his life. I will do *whatever* it takes for that to come to fruition."

Wouldn't that just be the perfect fairy tale? To actually be able to share her life with the man she loved as well as the child he gave her? This wasn't about her, however, and after this little escapade she'd be lucky to let Sean go to school without her on his six, hovering like a pissed-off mama bear.

"You don't spend time with your sister and her family because you don't want to risk them. How is it I don't get the same courtesy with my son? You'd willingly bring risk to him?"

"Our son, Iggy. *Our* son, and that's totally different." He backed away and ripped his hat off, raking a hand through the dark locks. "You're forcing me to make a decision between my son and work."

Maybe she was. "I'm protecting my son."

"And you think I'm a risk to him." Beckett crossed his arms, glaring at her.

"Not intentionally. I didn't have any intention to get snatched by DeSalvo, either, but damn it, Beckett, we've spent years tracking down and taking out powerful people. Evil people. Ones who want revenge. Sean's life is the most important thing to me. I will do *whatever* to protect him."

"I won't be pushed to the side because of my job, which I might not even have anymore because of what I did to help *you* out."

"Oh, hell no. Don't put this on me. You made your own decisions. You could have said no."

He materialized right before her again, hands gripping her shoulders, fingers digging into flesh. "Do you really think I'd let you face this alone? If you'd told me sooner, I would have been in his life from the very beginning."

Be honest with him. "No." Why did his touch singe her so?

"I want one thing, Iggy. I want to hug my son and hear him call me Papa." He lowered his head so his lips brushed the corner of her mouth. "And I'll be damned before I let you or anyone else take that from me."

Well, shit.

• • •

Aboard the jet, she crossed the floor in her private room, heels making no noise on the thick gold carpet, turned on her computer, and touched a button. After staring at her reflection in her compact, she put it away in her expensive handbag then sat in her leather chair.

Clicking the icon in the corner, she waited while the archived message was reencrypted with an unsymmetrical code, one unique to the thumb drive she carried with her at all times. Once it rested securely on her drive, it vanished from the computer as if it never existed. With a slight gritting of her teeth, she read the information, then closed it.

After removing the drive, she plugged it back into the gold heart around her neck. She sent out a few emails, then left the computer and the room to focus on the men in the Lear with her.

"Is everything ready?" one of the men asked.

"There's one final piece required." There were grumblings, and she hid her distaste. "That is currently being obtained."

"So no problems, then?" The same man spoke as looks were shared among them.

She rose and fixed herself a drink, not offering them one. She was no fucking flight attendant or woman to serve their needs.

"I am not a fan of the disrespectful tone," she warned. "You are guests on my plane as a courtesy for Mr. Red. I do not answer to you, and you would do well to remember that."

"Just as you should be aware *we* will do whatever necessary to ensure our cause."

She reclined in her seat and drank slowly, tamping down her craving to toss them out the emergency exit.

Chapter Eleven

Indigo held the butt of the rifle to her shoulder. Down the hill, the village snaked through the hills. All she had to do now was wait for the car carrying her target to come by. Three hours.

"Settling in?"

Beckett's deep voice flowed from her earpiece to warm her. Breaking the concern she had. It was always there lingering in the background. The chance of being discovered, of having her shot go off and killing an innocent. Shaking her head, she shoved those emotions back into a box where they belonged. If she focused on failing, she'd make a mistake. And she couldn't afford a single one.

"I'd be part of the ground if I was any more settled."

"At least it's not raining."

"Like the op in Costa Rica," she said, recalling it with clarity. "Spent hours lying prone in the rain just waiting for that one moment."

"That sucked. But right now, I'm comfy in bed."

A smile flitted on her lips unbidden. "You do prefer your comforts."

"Better when you're with me."

She rolled her eyes, the familiar banter calming stressed nerves. He'd always been a flirt on missions, claiming it kept her from worrying. He'd been right about that. The difference this time was no one else was listening in, as tended to happen on ops.

"Trust me, Beckett. I'd rather be with you in bed instead of lying out here."

"Really?" His amused tone had her chuckling under her breath. "Do tell."

"There are snakes out here, for one."

"Babe, believe me, there's a snake in here, too."

"Confident, much?" She checked the scope again. Nothing coming toward her. She was secure. "And stop that cocky-ass grin."

"How'd you know?"

"I know *you*, Beckett."

"Yes, you do. Don't forget, Iggy, that knowledge goes both ways."

"Not quite."

He grumbled under his breath. "How do you figure?"

Another check, and she flipped the night vision lens for the scope down as the sun lowered behind the hills. After spying the time, she replied, "You've continued being an agent for these past eight years. Me? I became a mom. I'm *not* the same person anymore."

"You might want to believe that," he said in a soft tone. "Don't tell me you've forgotten all those nights, lying naked in bed, in *my* arms and talking until sunrise."

That was the problem. She hadn't.

She steered the topic back to safe ground and Beckett, thankfully, went along with it. He was in her ear the entire time she tracked the car snaking its way through the winding road. Indigo steadied her breathing, closed her eyes briefly and lined up for the shot. Everything else faded into the background. This was just her and the gun. She curved her finger around the trigger, the metal cool against her skin, and fired the shot that sent his car tumbling down a ravine. Beckett stayed with her as Marco, again dressed as a paramedic, covered him with a sheet and shook his head to the onlookers, then dragged the body up the hill and into the back of the emergency vehicle, and drove away. Then and only then did she leave her position, ensuring no trace of her lingered, and she slipped off, blending into the darkness with ease.

He talked to her as she jogged the five miles through the countryside until he met her in a vehicle, and she slid onto the cracked vinyl seat, finally allowing herself to close her eyes and breathe in relief.

"I get you're tired," he commented.

"But you found something."

"I've eliminated the list of secretaries down to ones who've been around since before the items were stolen."

She sat up and rubbed her nape, trying to get it to loosen up. "How many?"

"Ten."

"I swear I don't remember seeing that many secretaries when I was there."

"Like you said, they have a knack for blending. I figured

you'd want a shower and clean clothes before we got on our way. I'll drive, giving you time to work the computer."

A shower sounded heavenly. "Good plan," she uttered, closing her eyes once more.

She woke at the sound of a ringing phone. She grabbed it and answered, "Yes?"

"Your clock is running out."

She pointed to the computer, but Beckett already had it up, tracing the call. "I just finished one. Only Fuentes is left, and as soon as I finish dressing, I'm heading back to the U.S. to handle him."

"Not asking how your son is?"

And give him the pleasure of not telling her? "I figured you were keeping him safe and sound because we both know what the future holds if anything happens to him." She determinedly ignored the guilt and fear his words caused her. Indigo fisted her hand then forced herself to relax, unwilling to let this bastard know he was getting to her.

"What did I tell you about threatening me, Indigo?"

She clenched the phone in her hand as she found Beckett's gaze. He gestured for her to keep him on longer. "Trust me, DeSalvo. This is not a threat. If my boy dies, then I have nothing to live for, and I'll be coming after you."

His laughter didn't settle her nerves. "I knew there was a reason the head of EGIS, Michael, liked you."

"You'd be wrong. He doesn't particularly care for me at all." A bead of sweat trickled down her spine as images of Sean lying dead flashed through her mind. She shook her head and pushed it away. She couldn't let him rattle her.

"Are you so sure about that?"

"The man's after me because he thinks I stole from him."

Beckett gave her a questioning look. "Why do you think he cares?"

"A hunch I have."

"Okay. You said before you had something else for me. What is it?"

"Right, I was wondering when you would get around to asking me about that. I have to go—wouldn't want you to be able to trace my location. I will let you know. Just remember, when people fall from their pedestals, they tend to knock off the lower ones as well on their way. Be cautious of those above you."

He was gone. She ended the call and sat beside Beckett.

"What was all that about?"

"He knows Michael was my boss at EGIS. Correction, he knew he was the head of EGIS. Think about this—if he knows who the head is, imagine what he knows about you. Your sister and her family."

Thunderheads filled his gaze.

"Where is he? He assumes I'm tracking him but wouldn't have enough time to get a lock on him. Glad for whatever my father did."

"He's back in Mexico." He held up a finger. "But he placed a call to someone in the States."

"Where?"

"That's where I didn't get the lock. It's a disposable cell and all that pinged for me on it was the northwest part of the country."

"I think," she began, "we have a bigger problem than we first realized."

"I agree."

"We can't just limit it to secretaries and janitorial. We

need to check out the higher-level agents as well. Pretty much anyone who's been around since I was." She opened the lid and pressed the power button. "I'll cross-reference them with Richard Chisom, DeSalvo, and anything else that pops up in my mind. And Duke Randolf."

She began typing and reading the files that scrolled along the screen. "Wait a second," she muttered.

"What'd you find?"

"Duke isn't just Chisom's best friend. Or was. Also, remember, he worked at EGIS as well. Didn't last long, but he was there. Held a janitorial position." She shook her head. "Odd thing is that this information had been erased."

"How'd you find it, then?"

"My father's program pulls up stuff people assume is deleted."

"Did any of them have anything to do with Michael?"

"Nope, he wasn't in on their hiring. That was all done through HR, vetting and everything. He wouldn't have spoken to them except if he said 'hi' in passing." She wiped her hand under her nose. "Chisom worked mostly with Markston and Fleurty. It mentions he'd also been paired with Akerson and Stackpole."

"They're dead." He peered briefly at her. "All of them are."

"Exactly," she commented. "A bit of a coincidence that each one is gone so we can't talk to them."

"How'd they die?"

"According to this file, an op went bad."

"What op?"

She read further. "Something in the Arizona called Operation Hawkeye."

"I remember that one. It dealt with domestic terrorism, a group called…"

"The True American."

He snapped his fingers. "That was it."

"I need to do some more reading. Are you okay driving?"

"I got this, Iggy. You figure it out on that end."

• • •

Beckett stood with Marco as the Little Rock cops finished up their work. The ambulance carrying the dead body of Jorge Fuentes had already left, and the two of them were standing among the lookie-loos.

"That was close," Marco said.

"They always are." In his mind, until he laid eyes upon Indigo once more and assured himself she was okay, close didn't begin to cover it.

"I'm heading off to help Lisa with the transfer. Do you need us for getting Sean?"

"Not that I'm aware of, but thanks." They had to wait now, DeSalvo had said. After Indigo took out Fuentes he'd call her, so until that call arrived they couldn't do anything about their son.

"You got it. You need anything, you call." He strode off, weaving in and out of the crowd until he disappeared from view.

Beckett wanted to run back to the hotel and wait for her. The city had been locked down as they searched for the shooter. Above, helicopters circled.

He wandered away, only to freeze when he spied a familiar face. Across the street, not looking in his direction, but he'd know the man anywhere. What the hell was Michael doing here? He stepped into the shadows of the building and continued to watch.

For once, Michael wore a suit and spoke with other men in suits.

Indigo's words about coincidences came back to him. He didn't appear to be looking for anyone, but then Michael wasn't anyone you'd expect to be the top dog in a clandestine organization. After shaking hands, the three men walked off in different directions, Michael moving away from Beckett and the way he needed to be heading.

A fourth man swung in behind Michael. Beckett frowned. Bodyguard. What was he expecting out here? Not a lot happened in Little Rock. Part of the reason Jorge Fuentes had picked it, kind of an out-of-the-way location.

Beckett wanted to follow him, but something kept him back. An intuition or gut feeling. Whatever it was, he was relieved when another man began following.

He was cautious as he returned to the hotel, taking extra twists and turns, making sure no one was trailing him. Indigo waited for him there, reading a book, their bags packed at her feet. Her right foot tapped, and he doubted she noticed. She hadn't received the call and the waiting was eating at her.

"I saw Michael," he said once the door closed behind him.

She closed the book and asked, "Here?" Suspicion spread across her face.

"Yes. He was with a few other men. No indication he was looking for us. He has a bodyguard and someone else following him."

"Are you calling him?"

"No. We have a small window to try and reach this Duke guy and get what we can before our next contact with DeSalvo. Let's go."

• • •

Beckett lay on his stomach, stretched out in the leaves, twigs, and needles strewn along the ground. He tracked Indigo's movements through the scope on top of his Kate, or Bravo 51. It had a suppressor on the end, and he shifted his weight and continued tracking her progress. The Kate wasn't his favorite sniper rifle, but it was damn accurate.

Figuring they'd have a better chance one-on-one, he and Indigo had split up; he'd stay hidden and cover her. Maybe Duke would be less likely to shoot a woman on sight. Hopefully.

He blew out a breath and scanned the area around her. Nothing out of the ordinary.

Everything had been different with Indigo as a partner. Right from the start, he'd felt a deeper connection with her than he'd ever experienced with anyone else. She didn't run from danger but toward it. She stood beside him and could more than hold her own. He respected the hell out of her and over time, it had changed into love. The best partner he'd ever had. Period. Bottom line. End of story.

Now, however, all that protectiveness and selflessness she'd had—her willingness to sacrifice herself for her country, friends, or partner—had been narrowed to one seven-year-old boy. Her son. *Their son.* His lifestyle did endanger Sean.

Regardless, it didn't give her the right to dictate if he'd

be allowed to be part of Sean's life. The boy was both of theirs, not just hers. The decision making wasn't in her hands alone. He had a right to be part of that child's life, whether or not he was part of EGIS.

She knocked on the door and stood to the side so he'd have a clear shot. Beckett held his breath as it swung open. The man who answered had hawkish features, a head of salt-and-pepper hair, and skin tanned from being outdoors. His thin, wiry frame didn't fool Beckett, confident the man could easily pose a threat. The scowl on his face wasn't exactly one of welcome. One squeeze of the trigger, and she'd be safe. He blew out two sharp breaths and calmed himself. Waiting for her signal or to see the danger himself.

"What do you want?" Beckett read the man's lips.

Indigo had turned to the side; he couldn't read her lips, but she was out of the line of fire.

"I don't know what you're talking about. Turn around and leave," the man said.

She shook her head and said something else.

"Don't make this ugly, girl. Get out of here while you can."

Beckett had forgotten how quick she was. Indigo moved, and the man's sidearm clattered down, and his heart seized when they fought hand to hand. He swore at not having a clear shot.

He grinned as she dropped low, leg sweeping out and knocking her opponent to the ground. She was on him before he knew what happened. The sun glinted off the silver rings on her index and middle fingers of the hand holding the serrated black tanto she'd had strapped to her back that now rested against the thin man's throat. Should have known better. She might have been out of the game for a few years, but it was obvious her skills hadn't faded.

When she turned her head in his direction, he read, "Come" from her lips. Scanning the area one more time, he pushed up from the ground and loped up to where Indigo had Duke on the ground.

"Covered." He held the rifle on the prone man.

Indigo rose in a smooth motion, simultaneously replacing her knife in the sheath. "Should have just agreed to talk to me, Duke. It didn't have to get ugly." She shook her head. "Get up. Don't think I won't kill you if you make a move."

"Or me," Beckett added.

"What the fuck do you want?" Duke spat, slowly getting to his feet. "How the hell did you find me?"

"Let's go inside," Beckett said, gesturing with the rifle's barrel.

Duke glared at him but nodded. Both men passed her, then Indigo brought up the rear, drawing the door closed behind her.

It was an old cabin, dusty and dilapidated. Light strained to make it through the windows covered with layers of dirt, grime, and newspaper. A single table with two rickety chairs under it, a couch that had definitely seen better days, and a table covered with containers of partially eaten food.

How the hell had the man gotten to living like this?

Indigo shook her head and slipped through to check the house. Duke's scowl deepened, but he didn't say a word.

Beckett breathed a bit easier when she returned. "Anything helpful?"

"Just more crap." She skirted a pile of clothing. "Looks like Duke here has a problem with minorities and the government."

"Bitch!" he bit off. "Don't need you touching anything and fouling it."

"Sit down and shut it." She took a pen and lifted some papers littering the table, sifting through without actually touching them. "I'm looking for Richard Chisom." A shrug. "We're looking."

"Don't know him."

Indigo turned a chair and sat on it. Pulling a knife, she used the tip to clean beneath her nails.

"You don't scare me, bitch."

"I'm not trying to scare you. I have dirt under my nails. I want to know where he is. Don't give me bullshit about not knowing him or him being dead. Everyone in here knows you worked for EGIS for a brief time. We also know you were, or are, well acquainted with Richard Chisom. I really don't have a lot of time to waste." She returned the knife to its sheath and rested her arms on her thighs.

It was all show; she was close to losing it. He moved to her side and gave her the Kate to cover Duke.

"Ne'er heard of him." The man sounded petulant.

"Really? That's not what it says on the papers at EGIS." The color drained from Duke's face. She shifted, dragging her fingers along the barrel. "Says you know him. Now, I'm nicer than the ones who'll be following me. They're more of a shoot first, ask questions *never* group." She shrugged. "Hell, I'm nicer than this one with me."

He licked cracked lips a few times before the words popped free. "EGIS? You're from EGIS?" Watery blue eyes flicked between the both of them.

Beckett hid his grin. "Yes, we are. Don't make the lady ask again."

"She's no lady," he growled.

Beckett had him up from the chair in a heartbeat, slamming him back into the wall. "Mind your fucking tongue when you speak about her." He wanted to punch a hole through the man's face.

"You are so right, I'm not a lady."

Beckett closed his hand around the man's throat as he dangled. He lowered his head to Duke's and whispered something in his ear. Seconds later the air filled with the pungent aroma of ammonia.

Stepping back, the man slumped to the floor, and Beckett positioned himself to where Indigo had a clear shot again. "We'll ask you one more time. Where's Richard Chisom?" Ice laced his tone, and he crossed his arms.

"He'll kill me."

Beckett shrugged. "Him or me. Your call. I can make it last a long time, and you'll wish I'd never crossed your doorstep."

"I already wish that." There was no more defiance in his tone, only faint desperation.

He looked at his watch. "Five seconds to start talking."

The hairs stood up on the back of his neck, and he glanced to Indigo. Their eyes met and he knew. Someone was coming.

"I...I would have to get the information from my room."

"No way," Beckett said. "Talk."

The faint *whomp-whomp* sound of a helicopter on the approach reached them. Adrenaline spiked, and he readied to battle. Whatever was coming, it wasn't going to be good.

"We have to go." Beckett wanted the information, but they had to go. He walked back to Duke and crouched beside him, then choked him.

"Don't kill him, Beckett."

He scowled at her and dropped the unconscious man back to the wall. He stood and took the rifle from her. "Stop looking at me like that. He's not dead, although I'd be doing the world a favor if I'd killed him. Fucking bastard. Let's get out of here."

She stared at him for a moment. "I got Chisom's address from his room. But I must have tripped an alert, so I figure Richard is the one coming. Or his men. Either way, he's not far from here."

As one, they dashed for the door and the Jeep. Tossing the weapon to her as she ran to the passenger side, he jumped in the driver's side. She caught it easily and swung into the seat. The engine started immediately, and he spun them around, whipping up leaves and dirt as he tore off down the narrow lane that masqueraded as Duke's driveway.

They had a mile to go before hitting the two-lane paved road. A fiery explosion hit to his left, and he swore, gunning the engine, praying for more speed. In his periphery, he saw Indigo rotating in her seat and firing up at the pursuing chopper.

The ruts and holes made for a bumpy ride, and he wondered if they weren't airborne more than they were on the ground. Left. Right. He zigged and zagged, avoiding the return fire from the MD 520N helicopter.

"Hold on!" he called out as the pavement neared.

Jerking to the left, they skidded onto the asphalt, tires grabbing for any purchase they could snag, nearly going over the other side of the narrow mountain road. He gave it more gas and they tore off. Indigo swore and reloaded, continuing to face the rear.

"Get us out of here any way you can." Indigo's words came over the chopper and the engine of the Jeep.

"We need to get out of sight and hide until dark."

"You're driving," she said.

"On it." He peered at her, scowling when he saw the blood running down her cheek. "You got hit?"

"By a tree branch. Hurts like a bitch, but I'm fine." She spun in the seat and stared out the back. "I don't see them. If you can get off, get off."

Oh, he could get off all right, but he really needed to concentrate on what she meant—removing them from the road and into some hidden place.

• • •

Indigo sat on the Jeep's tailgate under a concealment net while Beckett stood between her legs, attending the cut on her face. The helicopter *whumped* overhead, but they wouldn't be found. The vehicle blended in perfectly with the landscape and unless someone was on foot and physically ran into it, they'd be hidden.

"You're getting pretty beat up here, Iggy."

She shrugged. The five branch whips on her face stung but weren't important. "You don't have to clean them. I can do it myself."

"Are you kidding? Why would I give up the chance to be this close to you? You're not prickly now."

"Prickly?" She pulled back and stared up at him. "How am I prickly?"

His grin released a slew of quivering in her belly. He

tightened his fingers on her chin, holding her immobile, and continued tending to her wounds. "When I'm fixing injuries, you're never looking to pick a fight. I like that."

She rolled her eyes but didn't say anything else. He was right, she wasn't. After he put on the liquid bandage, he added butterfly closures. Before she knew what happened, he'd kissed her. Once. Lightly, yet it hit her hard. Thankfully, she was sitting and didn't have to worry about her legs giving out on her. Always a threat when dealing with Beckett Hanson.

He waggled his eyebrows at her. "Any injuries elsewhere I could check? Under here?" He lifted the hem of her shirt. "Or here?" His fingers tugged out her waistband.

"Would you be serious?"

"Iggy, I've never been more serious."

"We have work to do."

He groaned, then sat beside her. "We're stuck here until the sun starts going down. I can think of a good way to kill a few hours."

She didn't need that reminder. All that time, and she had lovely thoughts on what she'd like nothing more than to do to him. With him. For him. And none of it with clothing on.

Ignoring the tightening of her nipples and the clench in her belly, she shook her head. "We need to figure this out."

His nose flared. "I'm willing to bet anything Richard is in on the theft and that Duke was, as well. He's the one who did the grunt work for Richard, who wouldn't risk recognition in town."

"Good point," she said.

"So what now? It's Richard and Julie in on it together? Formerly dead operative and the head honcho's secretary?" His tone laced with sarcasm.

Silence reigned between them for a few charged seconds as his words echoed around them. Their eyes were locked on each other, realization streaming in.

Shit. She'd not thought of that. Scrambling for the computer, she powered it up.

"What you said makes sense, and it won't hurt to check it out."

He leaned over her, his breath warm along the back of her neck. "Not a bit. Although I can think of much more enjoyable ways to enjoy the time we have waiting." A dramatic sigh. "But if you insist we work, fine. We work. Although the chopper is around, and they might be able to pinpoint our location if you use it."

She nudged him with her shoulder. The familiarity of his teasing helped calm her. She was uptight. This had to work or she'd be on the run with her son for the rest of her life.

"We have to stay focused, but damn it, you're right. I can't use it."

"Trust me, Iggy. I'm focused." He leaned close and nipped the shell of her ear. "One-track thoughts. Single-minded focus. Want me to tell you what I'm focused on?"

She swallowed hard. The lump in her throat refused to disperse. His magnetism nearly overwhelming, she closed her eyes and took several deep breaths to steady her pounding heart. Her lids fluttered as she tried her best not to give in to the longing and tilt her head to the side, offering him more access.

"I want to lay you back on the seat after I've tossed the bags down. Strip you bare and press kisses all over your skin. Lick each inch, nibble my way up and down your amazing body."

Her belly clenched, and she barely bit off a whimper. Biting the inside of her cheek, she continued to stare at the information she had on the people who worked for EGIS. She located the file on Julie.

Lord help her, Beckett smelled so good. She remembered nights and days when she'd smell like him, wearing his shirt or after hours of making love. All she wanted to do was help him toss the bags out and have the opportunity to relearn all the cut ridges and planes of his body once more.

It was never just once more when it came to this man.

Beckett removed the computer from her hands.

She blew out a breath and stared up through the netting, watching the chopper circle away, unable to pinpoint their location. "We need to be alert, Beckett. They could have sent in ground teams." Her comment was a last-ditch effort to keep him at arm's length. Why? She wasn't sure. It would be so much easier to just give in and accept what was before her.

He began moving the bags so there was room to use the remainder of the seat. "I know."

"Then what are you doing?" All she could envision was them naked, limbs entwined…

"We'll watch in shifts. You sleep, I'll take first watch."

She narrowed her eyes at him, uncertain of his motives. He turned his head, meeting her gaze. The heat she saw there had need crawling along her skin. Her breaths were shallow and fast as she tried to control herself. Biting her lower lip, she waited for him to make a move.

"Come on, readjust and swing around." His grin didn't make her feel any better. "Make no mistake, I want you. My cock is rock hard thinking about what it would be like to be inside you. But I can control my urges. You need rest first. You've always been better at dusk and noticing things. I've got first watch." He glanced at his desert camouflage Special Ops watch. "I'll wake you in three unless we're discovered before then."

Then he walked away to sit on the edge of the tailgate, his Bushmaster QR Patrol resting across his lap. One weapon she was fond of. Anodized black, it fired 5.56-millimeter NATO rounds with a select-fire action. It looked good on him.

She lay down so she could see him, not understanding why after all these years he had such a profound effect on her. There was something seriously wrong with her to be staring at his back and thinking how sexy it was, the way his black shirt clung to his skin, the curve of his ass. With a groan, she squeezed her eyes shut and tucked her head so if she opened them again, she couldn't see him.

An act that lasted all of five seconds. She pushed up to call for him, only to find him staring back at her over his shoulder. No words had to be spoken, and he scrambled over to her, gathered her close, and kissed her.

Indigo moaned as his tongue slipped into her mouth. She wrapped her arms around his neck and kissed him back with everything she had inside her. Nothing else mattered right now. They were stuck where they were, and this physical connection was what she needed. With him.

He cupped her breast and thumbed the nipple, causing her to squirm on the makeshift bed. Nipping at his lower lip, she moved her hands down to undo his pants. He fisted a hand in her hair with a growl when she curved her fingers around his shaft.

"Iggy," he rumbled.

"I need this, Beckett," she admitted. "I need you."

He made short work of her clothing and soon was sliding fully inside her. Her synapses fired as his touch hit her on a cellular level. She slipped her arms under his shoulders and dug her nails into his shoulders.

Indigo gave herself over to him fully, holding nothing back. They didn't speak, but he held her gaze the entire time, refusing to allow her to look away. She was falling in love with him all over again. That slammed into her at the exact moment she orgasmed, his kiss muffling her cry.

They curled up together, and she drifted off to sleep while he got dressed to keep watch. Who knew what was on the horizon for the both of them. If this was her last time with him, she wanted to spend it in his arms.

• • •

Indigo went from dead sleep to fully awake the moment he touched her shoulder. Casting her gaze upward, she noted the location of the sun.

"Ground group is on the way."

She rolled to a sitting position and shoved her Glock in the back of her waistband and then reached for her rifle, a Sako TRG M10. Twenty-three-point-five-inch barrel, bolt action, and firing .338 Lapua rounds. Oh, yeah, hog heaven. Instead of formal black, this one was desert tan, which told her it had been used over in the Middle East. Either way, she was pleased.

Hopping out of the Jeep, she looked to Beckett for the direction they'd be approaching from, which he provided.

"How many?" Her voice instinctively pitched lower.

"Small group. I saw six. Seems to be more mercenaries and locals, which could be a problem. They're more familiar with this terrain than we are. Heavily armed with a mix of weapons. Pistols and rifles."

She looked around for what she needed and when she spied it, she strode toward the edge of the concealment net. Right before she reached it, a strong hand captured her wrist, pulling her to a halt.

Glancing over her shoulder, she lifted her brow at the man restraining her. He didn't speak, just held her gaze. It said all and more than words would ever be able to convey. He wanted her to be careful. She gave him a small smile and stepped free of his touch.

She moved swiftly, taking care not to disturb any leaves or twigs, all her focus on what lay ahead. At the tree she wanted, she shouldered the rifle and began climbing. When she reached her destination, she wedged herself in so she'd remain concealed. She didn't have a ghillie suit, so she hoped they wouldn't be able to spot her. Sprawling along the branch, she put the scope up to her eye and adjusted. The men were closer than she'd believed. Slowly, she took in the area. It was more than one group—a few scattered and spread-out men were moving in from other directions. However, they wouldn't be an issue. They were alone, so with slow methodical movements, she dropped them. The suppressor kept her from alerting the others.

She'd just pocketed the final brass and was trying to figure out whom to take out first when a man walked beneath her. He was armed—a firearm on each leg and an automatic machine pistol slung over one shoulder—but didn't hold anything other than the toothpick he occasionally removed from his mouth. Dressed in woodland camouflage, he moved very cautiously without sound. In fact, she quite possibly wouldn't have noticed him had she not been policing her brass. Richard Chisom.

Chapter Twelve

Beckett pressed against the rough tree bark and waited. The men would be at their makeshift camp in no time. But so long as they didn't radio the position, they should be fine. Men on the ground they could handle. A chopper flying overhead giving away their position and shooting missiles at them would be more difficult.

He focused on the man approaching him. Withdrawing his knife to take him out silently, Beckett slowed his breathing and waited for the moment. He felt no remorse in killing the man as his blade slid across his neck—it would have been one or the other who died. It was his job to make sure that wasn't him.

He whirled around at the muffled sound of a body falling to the ground. Shit. He'd been so homed in on the man he'd just dispatched he'd neglected to keep aware of his surroundings. He crouched by the fallen figure and glanced up at the surrounding trees. Indigo was out there, but he couldn't see her and had no idea where she'd positioned herself. He was relieved she wasn't sighting down her scope to kill him. Mouthing the words "Thank you," he left the man there and went after the next closest one to him.

Working in a wide circle, he eventually ended back up at their camp beneath the net. As the last man he'd faced fell to the ground, he went rigid at a new sound. One he'd never forget. The sound of a bullet sliding home into the chamber.

"Weapons down and stand up."

Without making any sudden movements, Beckett did just that, taking care to hold his hands slightly out to the side to show he didn't have any weapons in them. Where was Indigo?

"Turn around."

Moving slowly, he did as ordered and found himself looking into the blank expression of the man he recognized from his file picture. Richard Chisom. Unlike Duke, this man screamed *danger*. Dark, assessing eyes watched him from below the brim of a tatty cap. He was older now, but fit. And had at least three guns—those were the ones Beckett could see.

"Who are you?"

Beckett shrugged. "Does it matter?"

A deep breath. "Not really. Did you leave Duke alive?"

"He was breathing all on his own when I left."

"What the hell are you doing in my Ozarks, and how did you discover I was alive?" Richard replaced the sidearm on his side then aimed the machine pistol strapped over his chest at Beckett. "Who talked?"

"Besides Duke?"

A tensing of his jaw. "The chopper said you had a woman

with you. Where is she?"

Beckett shook his head. "No clue." That was the truth. "She does her own thing."

"Who is it? Who from EGIS did you bring with you?"

"No one."

"So you don't know where your partner is, and you don't know who from EGIS you brought." He spat a stream of tobacco juice. "What do you know? Or should I just kill you right now and let the animals dispose of your body?"

"If you're going to kill me, tell me why you stole money and weapons from EGIS."

A twitch of lips that passed as a smile appeared, only to disappear swiftly. "He finally realized that his stuff was gone, did he?" Richard shook his head. "Michael is one arrogant son of a bitch." He shifted his stance. "So you admit you're from EGIS, at least."

"Never said I wasn't. I only said I didn't bring anyone from EGIS with me."

"How'd you figure it out? I left everything so it pointed at that bitch. She should've taken the fall. As for why I did it? There's always a war that needs weapons."

"You won't get away with it."

"Son, you're not in a position to take me in. We're miles from anywhere, and from where I'm standing, I've got the upper hand."

"Perhaps." He sniffed. "Perhaps not."

He narrowed his gaze a micro. "What's that mean?"

"Nothing really, just that from where I'm standing, I see a red dot on your chest."

Richard glanced down and swore. He froze and stared at Beckett. "Someone answer me out there. Find the one who has this bead on me and take them out."

"No answer?"

"Shut up, man."

Beckett did, just watched and listened as Richard tried repeatedly to get someone on the other end of his comm. It didn't work.

"Who has the bead on me?"

The man didn't beg, not that Beckett had expected him to. "I'm sure you'll see soon enough."

"I can still kill you."

"You can try. I'd suggest lowering the weapon, though."

"Go to hell."

The tree behind Richard exploded as a round buried itself in the trunk, shattering bark and fibers. Before either of them recovered, that unwavering dot had returned to settle over Richard's heart.

"Your choice. Next time won't be a warning shot."

"Who's the damn sharpshooter you brought?"

"Not anyone you want sighting down her barrel at you."

His brow furrowed. "Her? Her who?"

Beckett didn't speak, merely waited for him to figure it out. He did. Richard's face paled slightly before he recovered. Although he knew it was coming, there was no way to actually be ready for a gunshot wound.

It all seemed to happen in slow motion. Richard lunged to the side, ducking from the mark on his chest as he lifted his weapon and fired at Beckett. The bullets slammed into him and knocked him backward. One in the shoulder and one in the side. As the ground broke his fall, Beckett watched the man in camouflage dash toward the tree line.

He didn't make it. Another shot rang out, and he fell

hard before lying still. Beckett pushed up, grimacing at the pain and lurched over to the man they'd come for. Blood pooled around his upper legs, and his eyes were shut. Using the last bit of his own energy, Beckett removed the firearms from the man, then collapsed with the shock of being shot twice. Darkness swarmed him, and he succumbed without much of a fight.

• • •

Beckett went from out to awake instantly. He didn't move as he tried to figure out what the situation was. Last thing he remembered was taking two shots from Richard Chisom's pistol.

"Indigo," he gasped, trying unsuccessfully to sit.

"Easy, Beckett." Her soft voice reached him through the darkness, winding around him and helping him breathe easier.

She rested a hand on his shoulder—the uninjured one—and gave him a gentle squeeze. "You're going to be fine."

"Richard?"

"In the next bed."

"Light."

Seconds later a soft glow filled the room. Staring through blurry eyes, he sought Indigo. She walked into view carrying a glass of water. Dark blue BDUs sat low on her hips and she wore a tight white camisole.

Sitting beside him on the bed, she assisted him up and held the cup to his lips. "Drink slow." He took a couple of sips and struggled to keep the pain at bay.

"Are you okay?"

"Yes. Sorry I let him shoot you. I didn't mean for it to happen."

"He alive?"

"For now." She helped him to lie back down. "You need to get some more sleep."

For now. Did he want to know what that meant? "Did… did he talk? And how did we get here?"

She nodded. "He did. He admitted his contact was Julie. Gave that up to hopefully cut a deal. Apparently, she was in love with him and willing to do whatever he asked of her. Chisom, being the scum that he is, took advantage of her weakness. The confession is taped and ready for you to deliver it to Michael. You woke up enough to help me get him and you into the Jeep. I did like we always do—figured out a way." A slight smile. "Rest now."

That meant she was going after her son next. Beckett reached for her hand. "We need to talk about how we're rescuing Sean, Iggy."

Her smile seemed slightly strained before she leaned down and pressed her soft full lips to his dry cracked ones. Injured or not, his body reacted to the feel of her against him. He moaned, and she backed away. "Get some sleep, Beckett. Thanks for helping me."

He watched her until she sat on a chair between the two beds, facing them, and put a rifle along her lap, her focus mostly the bed beside him, which held Richard. Closing his eyes, Beckett allowed himself to relax, content she wasn't running again.

The next time he woke the first thing out of his mouth was a curse. Anger rose within him, and he sat up with jerky moments. Pinning his gaze on the person in the chair, he barked, "Where's Indigo?"

. . .

She tapped one long nail on the shiny table, the large cluster halo diamond ring on her finger glinting in the bright light. "Has this decision been cleared by all involved?" She met each gaze of the ten members occupying the room. "I do not see Mr. Red present or his vote by proxy before me." Mr. Red was her man, and he didn't do anything without her approval.

"Then you haven't heard." The question fell from the thin blue lips of one of two other women in the large boardroom. Her true name wasn't spoken; instead she was referred to as Queen. Regardless, *she* knew her true identity, whether they called her Queen or Madam. She also knew *all* their identities.

"Heard what?" She straightened her spine, despising not knowing something they might.

"Of Mr. Red's removal from the board?" She twirled her gold pen before placing it on the obsidian tabletop. "Or his demise?"

Drawing upon her years of experience, she kept her composure, ignoring the crying inside her body. "How did he die?"

"Execution style. He'd been shot before that. There's also proof of trying to heal him, then, for some reason, they decided to kill him."

Rage rushed through her like water over a class-five rapid. She reached for her cup and took a sip. "Very well, I'll see the decision is carried out." She pushed back from the table.

"Wait." One of the men held up two fingers.

She paused, arching a brow. "I have work to do." *Deaths to avenge.*

"We'll expect you to take his place."

"No."

Their shared looks informed her they were used to getting their way. "No?" Qiáng asked the question.

She gave him her attention. "Correct. I did what I did because it amused me, not out of loyalty to you or your ideals. Good day." She left, ignoring the daggered stares piercing her back. Their plan to control the country wasn't her interest. She wanted wealth; that gave her the power she craved. She'd done what she had for the man who'd brought her in, but with him out of the picture, whatever scheme they had in play would have to continue without her.

It was time to fade into the background with her money.

Only when she was alone did she allow her diamond-hard visage to crack. *Dead.* He was dead? She had to find out who had killed him, then retaliate. Although starting off with that bitch Indigo Grey would make her feel so much better. And she knew just how to do it.

Chapter Thirteen

Indigo sat on a bench staring at the sole link between her and her son, as if she could will it to ring. Nothing, not so much as a peep while they'd been after Chisom, and now, without that to occupy her mind, all sorts of scenarios played out in her mind. She pushed from the bench and went to sit in the Jeep, resting her head back, allowing the sun to try to warm the chill moving over her body.

Nothing, and she scrubbed a hand down her face, praying. She turned the key and left the parking lot; she had to leave before Lisa arrived. On the road, her heart caught as, in her periphery, the phone lit up. Had she not been seated her legs would have given out, so great was her relief. Heart pounding and tears burning her eyes, she yanked it to her ear. She nearly had to pull to the side of the road. The need to survive outweighed it, and she continued to put more distance between her and where the EGIS agents would be arriving.

"Where's my son?" Indigo demanded into the phone, her grip such that her knuckles pressed white.

She'd slipped away from Beckett while he lay recuperating in the hotel room, aware he needed to rest more from being shot. Indigo didn't have time to wait. She'd called Lisa, informing her of their whereabouts and what to expect when she got there. It was the best she could do. Maybe it would also give Beckett some help in keeping his job.

"I must say, Indigo. You continue to surprise me."

"My son?" Every nerve in her body pulled taut. "I did what you required of me. All of it. Tell me where I can pick up my son." She had no way to stifle the pleading in her voice.

"I must tell you something."

"What?" Her tone was sharp. She watched the computer screen set up in her passenger seat, waiting for it to home in on his location. Her breaths grew more strained with each passing second.

If the steering wheel had been a sharp object, her hand would be bleeding, she held it so tight.

"I took care of your son. The truth you seek is in a house in Wyoming. I do a lot of things people do not approve of. I make no excuses for my ways. It is how I live my life. But you—spending a chunk of your life working for those who undermine everything you stand for is wrong."

What is he blathering about? "So you're having a crisis of conscience?"

He laughed. "Not at all. I just believe in leveling the playing field. Plus, I despise being used."

Word games, puzzles, subterfuge. She hated them all right now. "So you want me to go to Wyoming?"

"You might want to go as soon as possible."

Anger overtook fear. "Where is my son?"

"The abandoned house down the street from you, you need to check there. As for your son, I'm in Texas with your boy. I'll call you in twenty-four hours with the where and when you can get him back. I want to make sure of Fuentes's death." He hung up.

She stared at the phone, tears stinging her eyes like jellyfish needles. Nausea churned in her gut.

"Lying piece of shit. You're in Mexico." She marked the address and began driving.

• • •

"What are you doing here?" Beckett sat up, ignoring the pain in his chest. "Where's Indigo?"

Michael lounged in the chair between the beds. Beckett looked over at the second one. Empty.

"Where's Chisom?"

"On his way back to EGIS headquarters." He crossed his arms and scowled. "You've really gone and fucked up, Hanson."

He cracked his neck but opened his eyes to stare at his boss. "Really? How so? I found a mole and gave you the man who took the items from EGIS. I'd say I did a damn good job. And you can forget about prosecuting Indigo."

"Why were you so sure she hadn't stolen the items?"

"Why do you care? I tried to tell you back in your office, but you wouldn't listen."

"Things are fuckin' different now."

He had no idea. "I know because I was with her in that

hotel room after the op in Tunisia. She wasn't out of my sight long enough." He swung his legs over the edge of the bed.

"Where are you going? We have some things to take care of."

"I have something to do."

"You're quitting because of a fucking mistake?"

This was way more than a simple mistake. He stared at his boss, realizing the man was just brushing it aside as he did everything he didn't consider important. "No, I'm leaving because I want to be with my family. If I don't go now, I won't have them."

"Them? You mean Indigo?"

"Partially." He got to his feet. "Now, if you'll excuse me, I have to track her down so we can rescue *our* son."

"Hanson," Michael called out as he reached the door.

"Yes?"

"I want DeSalvo. We're going with you."

"I don't even know where the man is. I have to find Indigo first."

"I know where he is."

Beckett whirled on his boss. "You know? Where the fuck is he?"

"I'll brief you in the air. Any other questions?"

He threw open the hotel room door. "Only one. What the fuck were you doing in Little Rock?" No point in asking why they didn't help rescue Sean. If EGIS wouldn't go after one of their own, no way they'd go after a kid.

A slight twitch in the corner of his eye. "Need to know."

"You will not arrest Indigo when we find her." Cleared or not, he didn't trust Michael to not slap her back in irons.

"I thought you said one fucking question."

He nearly snarled at the man who'd been his boss for so long. "That was no question, Michael. *That* was a statement of fact." He left the room. His body ached from the injuries, but he ignored them. Only one thing mattered right now— finding Iggy and rescuing Sean.

Outside, he spied a large black SUV that screamed *government issue* all the way around. He gave a sharp nod to the man by the driver's door and slid in the back. Michael took the passenger seat.

"Airstrip," Michael barked once he was in.

A helicopter awaited them there, and Beckett shook hands with Selig. At least the wound was in his other shoulder. The pilot gave him a look he knew was more sympathy than anything. *Shit, I'm an idiot.* "Give me five minutes," he said, heading inside to the bathroom.

Once there, he locked the door and pulled out his cell phone. Cursing himself for his stupidity, he dialed Indigo.

"What do you have?" she asked the moment she answered.

"Where the fuck are you, Iggy?" He clenched the side of the sink, trying to calm down enough so he didn't rip it off the wall.

"Beckett?"

"Yes. Beckett. You left me in that room. Where. Are. You?"

"In Mexico, getting Sean."

There were days he wanted to strangle her. "You didn't think I'd be interested in coming along?"

"I wasn't thinking about you at all," she replied with her brutal honesty. "I am focused on getting my son back."

"You'll wait before you go in." His words were laced with steel.

"Why?"

"Because we're on our way."

"*We* as in Michael? The same man who locked me up and jeopardized him the first time?"

"EGIS has resources. I'm about to get in the air. We'll be there, just give me some time."

"How do you know where he is?"

He tugged the collar of his shirt. "Michael."

Her pause was all too telling. "You have until dark tomorrow." She ended the call.

Beckett swore, shoved his phone back in his pocket, unlocked the door, and walked out. He hastened to the waiting bird, climbed in, and slapped on a headset. "Let's get going," he said into the microphone.

• • •

MEXICO

Indigo held Michael's angry gaze. The tension was so thick between the two of them, Beckett would swear he saw sparks arcing and bouncing off the interior walls. She didn't flinch. Beckett had no doubt she was as pissed as Michael was, if not more so.

He rubbed his chest; the ache lingered. And his healing gunshot wounds hurt.

"You stay here," Michael barked.

"Fuck that," she retorted, slapping a hand down on the table. "You weren't able to get DeSalvo for years because your own secretary was tipping him off. I'm not exactly confident in EGIS's ability to wrap this up, and especially get my son back in one piece."

"That was a mistake with Julie, but we'll get him."

Michael gestured, and two men stepped forward. Well-armed men.

"They'll keep you company until we return." His angry stare focused on Beckett. "*You* have some explaining to do as well. Could have said you'd called her."

He was unmoved. "Not really." He slammed his pistol home. "She should come with us."

"Not a chance." He gestured toward the helicopter. "Let's go."

Beckett took a final peek at Indigo. She sat stiff as a board on the chair the two men, Joe and Artie, had put her. He had no doubt she'd be escaping these two.

"There is a seven-year-old who is *my world*. Be careful you don't get him killed." Her words were clear and crisp, no hint of any emotion.

"Move out, Hanson," Michael barked.

Beckett followed, trying to convey to Iggy he'd do everything in his power to protect Sean. If she picked up on it, she didn't let him in on it.

• • •

Indigo sat stewing in a small corner of the building she couldn't get out of without bypassing the men in the structure with her. She'd already picked her cuffs and had been trying to figure out the best way to escape. She was held in something akin to a closet with the door off while they hustled around the rest of the small space, not paying her any attention.

The phone at her side rang, adding a blue glow to the dimly lit room. She flicked her gaze to the men, who continued whatever they were doing, which didn't include her, because they never looked in her direction. Not the smartest of men, for sure, but perhaps they had her filed under "helpless female."

Her heart thundered faster. DeSalvo. Had something gone wrong? Had something happened to her boy? "What?" There was no way to disguise the panic in her tone.

The first sound to register was gunshots. Automatic and semiauto. Fear unlike anything she'd ever experienced, including when her son had been kidnapped, swarmed her. Had she been standing, she would have collapsed. Her head spun with the possibilities of what was going on at that end of the phone. What if she never saw Sean again? Never held him in her arms. Nausea churned and burned the back of her throat.

"Is someone there? Sean?" she called out. "Answer me."

"Say good-bye to your son, bitch."

"What's going on? I've done everything you asked." Tears leaked free. "You said you'd call and tell me where my son can be picked up. Damn you!" she cried, uncaring if the others could hear her. "Keep your word. Give me my son back."

"EGIS is raiding my compound."

"And you think I'm working with them? I'm nowhere near wherever the hell you have my boy!" Panic flooded her as she realized he no longer sounded like the egomaniac who could play a well-mannered gentleman. No, this was the man who had no problems setting fire to a schoolhouse—with the kids inside—just to prove a point. "If I was working with EGIS I would've been there, and we'd be face-to-face. Leave my son out of this, DeSalvo. He's done nothing wrong."

"I don't think so."

The call ended, and she roared with the fury of a mother whose baby was in danger. She tossed the cuffs and went straight to the base op room. The two guarding her had abandoned their post for some stupid reason.

Marco talked fast as she approached, weapon drawn.

"Where did they go?"

His eyes widened as he glanced at her before turning back to his screens and talking again.

Narrowing her gaze, she moved closer. "One final chance. Tell me."

"I'm a little busy," he snapped. "We're under fire."

"No shit. And my little boy is in the crossfire. So I'm not asking again. Tell me where they went or I'll kill you and find out myself."

"Shit! I'm hit! I'm hit!" The words came blaring out of the headset Marco had removed.

She recognized Selig's voice but never wavered from her position. "Time's wasting. Tell. Me. Where. They. Went."

The man shook his head, only to send her an apologetic look. The cold barrel of a pistol jammed in the back of her head. "Drop it, Indigo."

Hands out, she allowed her Glock to dangle as if she were about to give it over. The man behind her, Joe, reached for it, and she exploded. In a flurry of moves, she had him incapacitated on the floor and was lunging toward Marco. She clipped him in the temple with the butt of her Glock, and he went down as well, but not before delivering a well-placed hit of his own. All it took was looking at the screen, and she had the address. Two of them. She'd take the closest one first.

She grabbed some weapons from the room and shouldered her bag, then ran down the stairs, taking out Artie, who guarded the door. Out in the night, she scanned the street and grunted when she saw where she needed to get. Michael always loved his close ops, in case they needed assistance.

Running to her destination, she carried an Israeli-made Tavor-21 assault rifle fitted with a forty-millimeter M203 grenade launcher in her right hand. Over her shoulder, she had an HK MP-5K with the standard thirty-round magazine. Extras with her. And she also had her sniper rifle. Not her usual one, but a 12.7-millimeter VSSK, a Russian-crafted, silenced sniper rifle that took a large caliber. Normally referred to as a Vychlop, it was designed for operations requiring silent firing and superior penetration to those in vehicles, hiding behind them, or wearing heavy body armor. Her rounds were armor piercing and came in a five-round box magazine, 12.7-by-54-millimeter special subsonic. Honestly, she wasn't planning to need all of them. But if she did, she had extras.

The sound of gunfire reached her, and she hesitated before barreling toward the warehouse to find her son. She shot those who got in her way as she dashed from room to room, floor to floor. No sympathy—everyone in there was responsible for Sean being in danger.

Alarms rang out, and she kept to the shadows as she moved down from the second floor of the old building. She paused at a window and peeked out. No sight of DeSalvo, but what she saw had her reaching for the sniper rifle. A few short puffs of breath and she squeezed the trigger, sending the armor-piercing bullet through the SUV one of DeSalvo's men hid behind as he took potshots at another operative.

The second he fell, Indigo moved on, sprinting when she

heard vehicles starting up. As she turned a corner leading to the back, she watched a car speed away. She knew deep down that's where her son was. A roar of anger surged. To her left, she spied one of DeSalvo's men, lifted her assault rifle, and shot him in the leg.

She strode up to him and put the muzzle in his face. "Where'd he go?" she demanded in Spanish. She wanted verification of the address she'd seen on the screen.

The man shook his head and cussed her out. Her smile turned feral. "Do you really think I won't just pull the trigger and kill you?" She moved forward and put her foot on his wound, grinding down. He gasped, and pain filled his expression. "Where?"

He glowered at her.

She lowered the muzzle of her TAR-21 and put it against his crotch. "Will you tell me now?"

"Let him go, Indigo."

Michael's voice had her snarling. She remained focused on the man bleeding on the ground. "Tell me?"

More of that extremely unpleasant language, so she shrugged, then squeezed the trigger. The man screamed in agony as she turned to find Michael standing there, looking a bit green himself.

"Get out of my way, Michael, or I'll do the same to you."

"I can't let you leave."

She glared at him. "You don't have the resources to keep me. You fucked this up and that lunatic—who is now pissed off—took my son. I won't tell you again. Get out of my way."

He raised his arm, and all she noticed was the pistol in his hand. She reacted instantly, shooting him in the shoulder. He yelled as the Sauer fell from his fingers. "You shot me."

"Get it checked out. You'll be fine. You're lucky I didn't kill you."

She turned and ran until she found another one of DeSalvo's men. This one had seen what she'd done to the other and didn't waste any time divulging the information to her.

Armed with what she needed, she headed for a truck, only to draw up short when she saw Beckett standing there, blocking her way, sweat on his face, his expression furious, and looking like the man who'd battled at her side so many times.

Chapter Fourteen

Beckett didn't allow her any time to speak, just lifted his assault rifle and fired past her. She turned to see another man falling to the ground. He jerked his head to the side. "I've got a much faster ride over there."

Indigo slipped past him, grabbed the bag that she'd placed on the bench seat, and gave him a head motion to mean, "Get moving." Readjusting his grip on his M16, he led the way.

He'd taken possession of a sports car; the keys sat in his pocket. Once he saw the one tearing out of there, he'd swiped the keys to this one.

She opened the driver's door, tossed her items in the back, and slid behind the wheel to the passenger seat. He hopped in, gave her his weapon, and put the key in, bringing the engine roaring to life.

She didn't speak, and he observed her in his periphery. The set of her jaw, the determination in her gaze. Nothing was going to stop her. Or him.

"Where are we going?" He shifted lanes, asking for more speed from the car.

She placed his M16 on the floorboard between her legs. "He has another house he likes to hide at. It's about a hundred miles away. The one on your map marked with the red circle."

"How much of a lead does he have?"

"Fifteen to twenty minutes, maybe? He's in a fast fucking car as well."

He rolled his shoulders and settled back into the seat. They couldn't make that up, but they could keep it at the same interval. "I'm sorry."

She cracked her neck and settled back into the seat. All an act, because the tension radiated off her in waves. "Did you make the decision to rush in like an idiot?"

"No."

"Then you have nothing to apologize for."

He glanced at her. It took a lot for her to say such a thing. "What'd DeSalvo say to you?"

"He acted as though he knew I was working with EGIS." A slight tremble of her hand. "I'm done playing by any rules, Beckett. Any but my own. He's flipped. Sean is in danger, and I'll do anything to get him back."

Anger toward his boss surged through him. Yes, it was about the bigger picture, and that rarely included innocent civilians. This was different. Sean was his son. His child. The son of the woman he loved. Beckett had seen too many of the sick things DeSalvo had done to people, and it scared him to think of Sean exposed to him as well.

Sure, men like DeSalvo were allowed to remain free

because they occasionally turned one of their rivals over. That changed tonight.

He reached over and touched the back of her hand. "Let's go get our son."

He watched her as he spoke. Her reaction was slight, but she seemed to relax. Just the tiniest bit, but it was something. She closed her eyes, and he focused back on the road.

His cell rang, and he hit ignore. It rang again and again, both times ending with the same result. If she wondered who was calling him, she didn't say a word. The entire ride passed in silence.

She sat up when he slowed the car and shut off the lights.

This place was nothing like the warehouse from before. The building before him was massive. A well-guarded fortress.

Once he'd disengaged the overhead light and slipped out into the darkness, she opened the door. He followed suit and watched as she withdrew the bag she'd tossed into the backseat.

He moved to her side and took the NVGs she handed him. Slipping them on, he refocused on the grounds around them. His assault rifle in his hands, ready to defend them both.

"Beckett."

She barely spoke his name, yet he turned and caught the other weapon she tossed at him as if they'd never stopped working together. It was a well-oiled machine between them as they made their way down to the fence they had to scale.

"Front or back?" he asked.

"I'd love to level it." Her dry comment didn't answer his question, but he got it.

"Defeats the idea of a surprise attack." He nodded with understanding.

"Back."

He nodded and stared over the grounds, silent for a moment. "I've marked the cameras. We have a ten-second window to get over and back out of sight." He shouldered his rifle and took another look around.

"On your mark." She readjusted her bag, shook out her arms while he counted down.

"Five. Four. Three. Two. One."

They both took off for the stone wall and leaped for the top. He made it with ease. She didn't take much longer to reach his side and, with hand signals, he communicated what she needed to do once they hit the ground.

They dived for cover the moment they reached the ground. Two guards neared. He grabbed the first one, slicing the blade along his neck, killing him when the other fell.

Beckett glanced to his left and saw Indigo with a rifle up to her shoulder. She'd taken him out with a silenced weapon. He moved them into the shadows and dropped at her side.

His phone vibrated in his pocket. It rang again. And again. Swearing, he jerked it free and hissed into it. "Yes?"

"I've got infrared on your location."

Lisa. Beckett reached out and touched Indigo's arm, halting her. "Can you see in which room they're housing the boy?"

"Looks to be third floor, right corner. He's got another in there with him. It doesn't look good. Get in quick."

"Third floor, right corner. How many other guards on the premise?"

"Thirty to forty. Most inside in a common room. You

have twenty patrolling out—well, eighteen now. A few more wandering the halls. The majority are through the front and second door on the left."

Indigo handed him some wires: a headset for his phone. After plugging it in, he stowed the cell out of the way. He turned to tell her he was ready, only to discover he was alone.

"Shit. Do you see her?"

"Yes." Was that actual amusement he heard in Lisa's voice? "We both know where she's going."

She was after Sean. This was an all-out attack on her part; no one would be left alive if they got in her way. His hand closed over the bag she'd been carrying. He'd offer what she needed: cover. Watching her back.

"Talk to me, Lisa." He shouldered the bag and began to move. His ribs hurt, but he ignored the pain, which was secondary to getting his son out alive.

The closer he got to the house the more useless his NVGs, so he tossed them to the side.

He set charges around but didn't want to alert anyone to their presence until he had to. Until their son was safe with his mother. Lisa gave him periodic updates on Indigo between telling him where to go and how many men were approaching.

Although he'd been expecting it when that first shot rang out, he wasn't entirely ready for it. Not because he didn't know his job, but because for the first time it was his woman *and* his son in the mix.

"All hell's about to break loose, move!"

Bag dropped and the items from it spilling around him, he headed toward the house. He had to ignore the need thrumming through him to run all out; he was her best asset if he was a surprise.

The huge house mocked him as he pushed in. Keeping to the shadows, he inched to the door that had most of the guards behind it. He rigged the door and headed for the stairs.

More gunfire came from upstairs, but it was nothing compared to the explosion when the men tried to open the rigged door. Lights flickered and smoke billowed along with flames. He ran on—no point in hiding. At the top of the steps, he ducked to avoid the bullets whizzing past his head.

They volleyed fire between them, and he tossed the weapons away when they emptied. "How is she doing?" he asked as he slammed another magazine into his current gun.

"Fighting hand to hand."

"Where?"

"Third floor."

She was much closer than he was. Spinning, he fired as he moved from pillar to pillar. Wiping dust and sweat off his face, he continued on as man after man fell.

"Keep an eye on her."

"Keeping one on both of you. Get your ass moving." A slight pause. "Shit. You need to head back down. Men are pouring from the basement and heading up. Got to slow them down."

He cursed but scrambled back to the top of the stairs. Rigging a block of C-4, he shook his head. That ought to slow them. He wasn't going to sit and wait.

Beckett ran for the stairs leading to the third floor, cursing when a bullet tore along the outside of his thigh.

Locking away the pain, he pressed on. He ran past dead bodies and never slowed. Indigo would be fury unchecked.

He froze when he heard, "You sure you want to shoot your own son?"

"I won't shoot him, I'll just kill you." Indigo's voice fell flat and unemotional as she spoke to DeSalvo.

Beckett paused, waiting for the opportune moment to help. This was where he couldn't go busting in, not with Sean there. Edging to the corner, he peered in, and anger flooded him. DeSalvo was using the boy as a shield and held a gun pressed to where Sean's shoulder and neck met.

"You brought someone with you. Who from EGIS helped you?"

"I told you, I wasn't working with EGIS. This is because you reneged on the deal and took my son with the intention of killing him."

"I know Beckett Hanson is here. You lied to me."

"No. I didn't. He's here, yes. But not as an EGIS member. Beckett is Sean's father."

Beckett watched his son's eyes widen. Sean looked so scared. *Sean.* His boy. His child. He trembled with the enormity of that realization.

"So both father and mother watch their child die."

$$\cdots$$

Indigo knew Beckett was near. Right now, though, all her attention sat focused on the bastard holding her son hostage. She kept her gaze on DeSalvo, because if she continued assessing the bruised and battered condition of her precious boy's face she'd lose it.

She had her Vychlop in hand, currently leveled at DeSalvo.

"You're not killing my child," she vowed.

"Put down your gun, and we'll leave."

"I'm not letting you take him anywhere." She pursed her lips three times, blowing out breaths as she waited for the perfect shot.

"You can't stop me." His eyes were wild. The crazed animal that'd finally been cornered and realized there was no way out.

Her world narrowed to the place she wanted to send the bullet. "Close your eyes, baby."

"Your mother can't shoot me without hitting you." DeSalvo spoke loud and confident.

Indigo used her mother tone, which meant there was no room for argument. "Listen to me, Sean. Close your eyes, and we'll go home soon."

She didn't have to look to accept her son did as she'd asked. Sending up a prayer to make her shot dead-on, she pulled the trigger without remorse. It paralyzed DeSalvo before he knew what had happened. There wasn't time for his finger to pull the trigger. Before the Sauer he'd held on Sean hit the floor, the man was dead, his blood on her son's face.

Indigo dropped the sniper rifle and ran to her child, gathering him tight in her embrace. Tears flowed freely as he hugged her. She leaned back, wiped the blood from his face, and kissed him.

"I'm so sorry," she mumbled.

A hand on her shoulder had her turning to see what Beckett wanted. He stared at his son before meeting her gaze again. "We need to go."

She nodded. "Can you run, Sean?" She brushed some unruly, dirty hair from his face. God, his battered face broke her heart, and she wanted to kill DeSalvo all over again, this time much more painfully and much slower.

"Yes, ma'am." His voice quivered as he did his best not to shed tears.

"Let's get out of here then."

His big brown eyes moved to the man standing beside her. "You? You're my father?"

Beckett looked at him, his expression one of business first. "Yeah, kid. I am. Your mom is right. We need to go. We can talk after we get you safe."

"You're bleeding." A solemn statement from a boy who'd had to grow up far too quickly.

Beckett nodded. "I am."

Indigo got to her feet and picked up her rifle, keeping her free hand on Sean. "Which way?" she asked Beckett.

He was silent for a minute then nodded at a wall. "Lisa says there's a passageway there. It'll take us outside, and they'll have a ride waiting for us."

She didn't want a ride from EGIS, but she'd accept one from the devil in order to get her son to safety.

It took them a short time to find the passageway, and they were off. She began to lead, but Beckett shook his head at her, so they went with him first, Sean in the middle, and her bringing up the rear. Her Vychlop slung over her shoulder, she carried her TAR-21 for use in close quarters.

They ran into three people that he shot without hesitation. Each shot had Sean shaking. When he stumbled, she went to reach for him, only to have Beckett there, hefting him into his arms. "You're on point," he rumbled. "I'll keep him safe."

She began running again, and when they burst from the

hidden passage into the night, she breathed easier. Looking over her shoulder, she saw Beckett carrying Sean. Thankfully, the man kept her son's face pressed against his neck, hiding him from the carnage best he could.

"Where's this ride?" she demanded.

"Lisa?" he asked. "Ride?" He grunted. "Should be here in moments. She said we should hear it coming, and we can trust him."

Sure enough, she could hear chopper blades as they whirled through the air. She went to Beckett. "Got any more explosive?"

He nodded and handed Sean to her, then dived into the bag. It didn't take him long to rig the door to explode should anyone follow them. A large black bird lowered. Selig sat behind the controls of the UH-1 Iroquois helicopter. It was an old bird, but she was grateful to see it.

"Go," he hollered, taking her weapons from her and laying down cover fire as a group of DeSalvo's men burst onto the scene.

She followed his order, burying Sean's face against her and doing her best to keep him safe. Once she'd climbed in, she peered back in time to see Beckett tossing the TAR-21 when it emptied. A vehicle came tearing toward them. After lifting the sniper rifle, he fired at an oncoming car. He didn't hang around to watch the resounding explosion, just jumped in, yelling, "Go. Go. Go!"

Selig did, lifting them up and flying away. She didn't pay any attention to what was around her, just tightened her hold on Sean, burying her face into his hair. The tears flowed free again, and she didn't care. She snarled at Beckett when he tried to get her to release the boy.

"He needs medical care, Iggy," he said softly.

Taking the med pack from him, she took care of her son, wiping the blood off him and cleaning out his injuries. Sean's expression was vacant, and she shook her head, wondering how much damage she'd done to her child.

"I'm so sorry, Sean."

His tears were like shards of glass embedding deeply into her skin. She covered him with a blanket and tucked him in beside her once he'd been seen to. It didn't take long for him to fall asleep, the exhaustion, worry, and stress having taken a toll on his young body.

From lowered lids, she observed as Beckett put on a headset. He spoke, but she didn't care enough to pay attention. Possibly stupid on her part, but right now, Sean held all of her focus. She continually wiped the tears that leaked from his eyes, wishing they were anywhere else but here, where she could assure him he was safe and that nothing like this would *ever* happen again.

Powerful thighs clad by black BDUs appeared before her. She stared at the way they hugged his legs as Beckett crouched before her, headset gone. As was the earbud he'd worn when in communication with Lisa.

"How's he doing?"

"How do you think? We shot numerous people right in front of him—he had their blood on him." She rubbed her eyes, amazed by the amount of grit in them. Lord, she was exhausted. The mere fact Sean was back with her had her fear sliding away to be replaced with bone-wearying exhaustion.

Beckett looked from her to her son. Correction, *their* son. He reached out a hand and brushed some of the dark curls back from Sean's face. The depth of emotion there would have taken her to her knees had she not already been sitting. Part hesitation and part awe. 100 percent love.

"You need to get that looked at." She gestured at his leg.

He glanced at her and shrugged. "It will be."

Jerking her head to the other side of Sean, she said, "Sit. I'll take care of it."

Beckett did, stretching out his leg so she had access. Brushing a kiss over her son's forehead, she picked up the kit and maneuvered to Beckett's injured side. Just a graze, but it had to be painful. She made sure to keep her attention on his injury as she worked, refusing to look at him. It didn't take her long before she was finished.

"Thanks."

She nodded and had started to move back when he captured her wrist. Doing her best to ignore the wealth of emotions his simple touch created, she peered at him. She craved his lingering touch, the strength his embrace gave her. His amazing blue eyes stared back at her. Sparks arced between them and she swayed toward him, unable to help it.

He met her halfway, his firm lips welcome and familiar. She closed her eyes and opened for him. His tongue sweeping gently through her reminded her how tender he could be. This wasn't about anything other than relief that their child was safe and with them. The kiss ended almost as quickly as it began, but she'd swear during that short time, he'd recaptured her soul.

Beckett rested his hand along her jaw, his thumb tracing the line of her lower lip before falling away. Tears threatening, she backed away, settling herself on the other side of Sean. Her son snuggled safely between them both; she didn't fight when Beckett leaned her head on his shoulder.

Just a few moments of rest. They were in the air, and she could do with a catnap. She took one more sweep of the helo's interior. Selig at the controls and Beckett beside her. Son safe. Yes, things might not be perfect, but they were a damn sight better than when they'd stolen the car earlier. And while she hadn't talked to Selig since her *return* to EGIS, she trusted Lisa would make sure they were safe and went nowhere near EGIS or Michael.

• • •

Beckett stirred when the helicopter banked to the left. Opening his eyes, his gaze immediately went to the woman who had her head resting upon his shoulder. Her lashes, thick and full, settled upon her high cheekbones. Morning's early light spilled into the chopper, which allowed him to see her. Her skin, smudged with dirt, dried sweat, and blood.

Lowering his gaze, he spied the child wedged between them. *His son.* He'd wanted to hold him tight and keep him safe, but Sean had turned to his mother.

That would change, though. He was going to be part of his son's life. The more he watched the boy lying partially on him and partially on his mother, the more he could see himself in the young features.

He touched the black curls and allowed his hand to drift down his face, avoiding the bruising, which showed, no matter his darker skin.

Michael. That bastard had pushed this situation too far. Beckett understood with startling clarity why Iggy had run the moment she'd discovered she was pregnant. There wasn't anything that man wouldn't do to suit his needs, no matter who was a potential casualty. He'd kill the man when he saw him next.

Swallowing his rage, Beckett stayed as calm as he could. DeSalvo was dead. The man who'd done this to his boy no longer breathed. And soon, Michael would pay for his duplicity.

What would happen now? He refocused on Indigo Grey. In sleep she continued as the warrior, one hand wrapped around her sniper rifle and the other her son. *Their* son.

What had she been like pregnant? How had the birth been for her? Had they lived in other states before they settled in Wyoming? Part of him wanted to wake her and ask all those questions and more. Instead, he tipped his head to rest upon hers and closed his eyes again, allowing the illusion of family to continue.

EGIS was no longer the place for him. But how to provide for his family? What would he do?

Plus, if Iggy feared she was a target, why wouldn't he be one, too? He'd been active longer and more recently than she had. What dangers would he bring to their doorstep if he went with her and stayed as part of their lives?

He groaned and scrubbed a hand down his face. What the fuck was he supposed to do now? Maybe he needed to disappear and figure this all out first. To be the one to make the decision, as opposed to Indigo, who seemed extremely adept at telling him how it was going to be. At the same time, he had no wish to lose more time with his son. Still.

Distance from Iggy and Sean. Distance from the place that had been his home for so many years. That's what he needed most right now. But where to go?

The next time he woke, they were landing. A quick glimpse to Indigo had him smiling slightly. She and Sean both slept. Brushing his lips over her forehead, he slid free and stepped up to where Selig was setting them down.

Headset on, Beckett clapped the man on the shoulder. "Thanks for the pickup, man."

"Not a problem. Lisa told me you needed a quick out." A light lift of one shoulder. "I'd seen this and borrowed it. She also gave me coordinates of where to put you down. Told me to tell you there's a vehicle waiting and some money for you."

"Perfect timing." He owed that woman a case of whiskey. "What about Michael?"

Selig shrugged. "I didn't ask."

Which meant Beckett would have to call him.

"Lisa said DeSalvo was dead. Is it true?"

"Yes." He rubbed the stubble on his face. What he wouldn't give for a shower right about now. "Indigo killed him."

Selig grunted. "I don't know her well, but I have to tell you, she's one hell of a woman."

He found himself brimming and smiling with pride. "Yes, she is."

They bumped once before the helo settled to the ground. Removing the headset, Beckett pivoted on his good leg. Indigo and Sean slept. Outside, he could see a small gray Jeep Compass waiting for them.

"Indigo."

She barely moved. She had to be exhausted. He couldn't imagine what it was like to go through what she had.

"Indigo." He nudged her with his boot. That did it. She

reacted instantly, bringing the rifle up. "Easy, darling. We've landed, and we need to get going."

Her large brown eyes met his gaze. "Where are we?"

"A safe zone. Lisa set it up."

Beckett picked up her son and watched as she hopped to the ground. He followed, refusing to give up possession of his boy. At the Compass, he dug in his pocket as Indigo strapped in a sleeping Sean, while behind them, Selig lifted off.

Phone to his ear, he waited for Michael to answer.

"Where are you and better yet, where the fuck is she?"

He narrowed his eyes, longing to punch the bastard in the throat. "Out of your reach, Michael."

The man growled. "Perhaps you should take a little bit of time to reevaluate your priorities, Hanson. Get her out of your system, because you seem mighty confused on how this works. I want her here. She isn't cleared until I am perfectly confident Julie is the guilty party."

Beckett ended the call without a word. Confused was right.

"What happens now?" Indigo asked, her tone a bit sharp. "I need to get Sean home."

It grated on his nerves how she put him aside and didn't allow him to be part of the going home. He ground his jaw. "And you think I'm just going to let you take my son out of my life?" He prowled a bit closer to her as she pushed the door closed with one hip.

Her fingers flexed; she was ready to fight if necessary. A shaft of pain lanced him. After all they'd gone through, she didn't trust him?

"I don't want you around him, Beckett. I told you that.

Not so long as you're part of EGIS." She ground her teeth. This wasn't about her—it was about what was best for her son. "I'm willing to think about it, but I'm not kidding about EGIS. You *need* to be out."

He gripped her arm and propelled her to the passenger door. "You can't keep me from him."

"That's what you think," she muttered under her breath.

New anger flowed, and he slipped behind the wheel. "Where to?"

"An airport."

"And how do you propose to get tickets without IDs?"

"My father."

He started the engine and drove to the nearest road. The nav system said they were in northern Texas. Keeping his comments to himself, he drove to a restaurant a ways from where they'd landed.

He'd picked a place with outside seating and few customers, so their conversation was basically private. He crossed his arms while she picked at her salad and Sean wolfed down a burger. "You can't keep me away from him, Indigo."

She put her fork down and met his gaze, her own angry and defensive. "Don't bet on it."

"Half mine." He forced the words out from between clenched teeth as he pasted on a smile for the boy's sake.

"All mine."

He raked a hand through his hair. "Bullshit. He's my son as much as yours. Don't forget that."

"And don't you forget what *your* so-called family put him through just now." Ice coated her words.

"Mama?"

"Eat your meal, Sean," she said, meeting Beckett's stare. "*We're* going home soon."

He jerked to his feet and braced his hands on the table. "You really can be such a—" He clamped his mouth shut. Shaking his head, he reached in his pocket, withdrew a phone, and put a number in it. Then he gave it to Sean. "This is your phone, son. Anytime you need to get in touch with me, call me. Just dial the one under"—he slanted his gaze back to the mother of his child—"Papa."

Beckett reached over the table and gripped Indigo's chin, bent and kissed her. "This isn't over." Furious, he left the keys for her and stomped off. He had to figure this out, otherwise they'd be going around in the same circle forever.

Although it killed him to remain at a distance, he watched until they got back in the Compass and drove away. Then he went to the nearest pay phone and called for a taxi to take him to the airport. It was time to get clear on a few things.

Chapter Fifteen

After spending time with his sister and her kids, Beckett understood EGIS wasn't his family, had never been his family. It was no more than a job. He'd gone to have it out with Michael, but found himself here, behind the man in one of the EGIS interrogation rooms. Julie sat in the hard chair, her left wrist cuffed to a loop in the table.

Michael tossed a file on the table. "So, all this time, it's been you. You're the one. The one they call Madam. Or do you prefer Queen?" His tone was sharp with fury.

She held her former boss's gaze without emotion.

"Why?" Beckett asked. Everything they had on file about Queen impressed him. Private planes, stashes of cash, illegal weapons sales to insurgents, all conducted right under their noses. She was a cold, calculating woman with no remorse, and it showed now.

She shifted her attention to him, slow and with purpose. "He wanted the stuff." No remorse. Julie spoke with that same no-nonsense tone she'd wielded like a scalpel behind her desk.

"He, who?" Beckett pushed the issue.

A bored sigh. "Richard Chisom. You know all this. He confessed everything during your—*her* questioning of him."

"You have no rebuttal?" Beckett repositioned himself by the table's edge.

She angled her head slightly to the left before straightening it and staring back at Michael. "I've been doing what I do for over a decade. If you've found me out, why deny? I did what I did. Before you ask, no other reason than for love."

He and Michael exchanged glances of disbelief.

"Really?" Beckett fisted his hands and braced his knuckles on the table. "You did all this, risked everything including your freedom, because you were in love with a man who, the moment he was caught, gave you up without a second's hesitation?"

She turned pearl-gray eyes upon him. "That's odd to you?"

"Yes, along with incredibly stupid. He doesn't care about you. Why are you still protecting him?"

She arched a pencil-thin eyebrow. "I'll do whatever to protect the ones I love." She held his gaze. "Wouldn't you?"

He focused on the plural she used. Did she know about Sean? "You said *ones*. Who else besides Richard is in this mess?"

She touched her right index finger to the corner of her mouth. "You, who threw off years of dedicated service and risked federal incarceration because your ex-lover needs your help." Julie stared dispassionately at him.

"That's not what we're here to discuss."

Michael's stare bored into him, yet Beckett managed to ignore him.

"I saw it the moment I first saw you two on camera. You were infatuated." She gestured in Michael's direction. "Some were blind to it. Not me."

"What's your end game?" Michael rapped on the table to get her to look at him.

"I don't wish to speak to you. I'm talking to Beckett."

Beckett felt Michael's frustration in the air; it fairly vibrated with it.

"And tipping off DeSalvo? What was the point in that? You knew what he was capable of and what he did."

She pulled on the chain securing her to the table. "Always important to have morality-lacking people under your thumb. At your beck and call. Things don't get done, the necessary, dirty things, when all you have around you are people who righteously toe the line. Wouldn't you agree, Mr. Wythe? Easier to eliminate people like Duke." Anger leached into her tone for the first time.

Michael scowled at her.

Duke was dead? He'd been alive when they'd left him. He wanted to ask Michael, but now wasn't the time to ask it.

Julie's laughter reminded Beckett of Maleficent from *Sleeping Beauty*.

"Open your eyes, Mr. Hanson," she said reverting to her professionalism. "There's a lot more than you would ever believe that happens."

"We're done here." Michael picked up his file and strode to the door.

Beckett accompanied him, pausing at the opening to

peer back. Julie sat as if behind her desk. Ramrod straight
and perfectly composed. "Things aren't always what they
seem, Mr. Hanson. Don't forget that. This man knows way
more than he's letting on."

Michael slammed the door on her words with substantial
force.

What had she meant? Something else Michael was
hiding? "How did Duke die?" he asked as they strode off
down the hall.

"Let it go, Hanson. Need to know. Have some loose ends
to tie up." Before Beckett could say another word, Michael
had disappeared through a set of doors.

• • •

A packet lay on his bed. Beckett glanced at Lisa, who'd
walked with him to his room. He was done waiting for Michael to find time to see him. His bags were packed and already in his truck.

He wasn't exactly sure why it had taken him so long to
come to this decision, but he was grateful for Iggy and Sean
and planned to spend the rest of his life showing his love for
them. *They* were his family.

"What's that and where did it come from?" He indicated
the packet. There was no return address or any kind of
marking to identify it.

"No clue."

He opened it, and a thumb drive fell into his hand.

Lisa shrugged when he held it out, so he walked over to
his desk.

After clicking on his computer, he stuck the drive in and

stared at the files that flashed on the screen. It took him a few moments for it all to sink in. Michael's dealings. All the ones that were below the letter of the law. And not just a toe over the line, either.

"What is it?" Lisa asked from where she stood by the window.

He swallowed his anger. "Just some insurance." He shut down his computer and pocketed the drive. "Just some fucking insurance." It was the last straw.

On impulse, he hastened across the room, hugged Lisa, then stepped away. "Be happy, Lisa."

He strode to the elevators and took one from the EGIS living quarters up to the floor with Michael's office. His new secretary sat at the desk, young and brunette, and she smiled at him as he neared.

"Mr. Wythe is in a meeting."

"I don't give a fuck," he snapped, moving by her and thrusting the door open.

Michael was at his desk, reclining as he spoke on the phone. He narrowed his eyes at Beckett. "I'll call you back," he said, then disconnected the call. "What are you doing storming in here, Hanson? You were told I was in a meeting."

Beckett marched over and coldcocked him. "You selfish fucker. You deliberately put that boy—*my son*—in danger. You knew you were endangering a child. You knew the whole time. All to get DeSalvo." He reached for his floral shirt, yanked him up, and hit him once more, sending him flopping back into his chair.

"Stop hitting him," the secretary cried from behind him.

She was probably calling for security. He didn't care. Michael got to his feet, wiped the blood from his nose, and held his gaze. "Feel better now? Get it out of your system?"

"You're not even going to deny it, are you?"

"What for?" He looked at the back of his hand, then reached for some tissues from his desk. "Can't believe you hit me."

Beckett grabbed two fistfuls of his shirt and slammed him back into the wall. "I want to kill you," he vowed. "Slowly, painfully—excruciatingly so."

"It's nothing personal," he said, spitting a stream of blood to the floor. "It's part of the job."

"Wrong," he said in a low rumble. "It became personal when you dragged my son and his mother into the mix."

Michael held his gaze. "It's the job. Get over it."

The phone in his pocket rang, interrupting his response. Without looking at the screen, he snapped, "What?"

"Papa?"

Sean's scared voice tumbled through the line, and his world narrowed to only that. "Sean?" He blinked. "What's going on?"

"Mama…"

His heart thundered at the fear in his son's tone. "What happened, kid?"

"She's in the hospital. She…she fell and…and…and they took her away in the ambulance."

Dizziness swarmed him, and he locked his knees. "I'm on my way, Sean. On my way." He hung up, grateful he'd pinged the phone he gave to Sean and already knew where they lived.

Michael frowned. "You don't have time for them. You have a job here. A responsibility."

Beckett slugged him once more. "Fuck you. I see you

again, I *will* kill you. Don't come after me or us in any way. Or the proof I have on what you've done will become public. Julie might have been a mole, but she was smart and documented everything. If you interfere in our lives again, I'll blast it all over DC." He shoved away and pivoted to see two guards come barreling in. "Get out of my way," he snapped, punching one and pushing the other out of his way. His responsibility was to his son and the woman who owned his heart.

"Hanson," Michael called.

Ignoring him, he dashed to the elevator. He gulped down the nausea that rose with each step. What if he never got the chance to tell Iggy he loved her?

. . .

Indigo cracked open her eyes. A hospital room. That wasn't good. Where was Sean? What the hell had happened? The beeping from the monitors was the only sound she heard.

So weak she could hardly move, the most she could do was scan the room. She didn't see anything until she looked to the right.

There, sleeping in the chair, were Beckett and Sean. Slowly, she turned her head and gulped up the image of father and son. Both wore dark indigo jeans, and Sean had on his long-sleeved yellow dinosaur shirt, his favorite. Beckett's white shirt was a stark against his dark brown leather jacket.

Tears pricked her eyes, and she closed them.

The next time she opened them, only Beckett was there. Where was Sean? She dampened her lips and swallowed before attempting to call out to him.

Beckett opened his eyes as if he'd felt the weight of her stare. For a moment they remained like that, gazes locked on each other. He rose, then approached her.

His eyes were suspiciously bright as he cupped the side of her face. "God, Iggy. Don't ever do that again."

"When did you get here?"

"Late last night."

"Where's Sean?"

He kissed her. Once. Gently.

"Getting something to eat with your neighbor Dan Wilbon. I picked up Sean from the Wilbons' and came here. I promised Sean I wouldn't leave your side while he ate." Beckett dragged the chair closer and sat, holding her hand. "I know, Iggy."

She wanted to lay eyes on her child. Hold him. See for herself he was all right. "Is Sean okay?" She shook her head slightly. "You know what?"

"Sean's fine. He called me when you collapsed." He squeezed her fingers. "I know that you're pregnant with our next child."

It was a good thing she lay in a hospital bed, for that surely would have knocked her legs out from under her. "What?" Somewhere in the back of her mind, she recalled hearing that from a doctor, but she'd chalked it up to either a dream of wishful thinking or overhearing them say it to someone else.

He dragged his knuckles along the curve of her cheek. His gaze, gentle yet determined, never once wavered from hers.

"We're having another baby." He kissed her fingertips. "I was so fucking scared when Sean called me. And I have to tell you something."

Her mind wouldn't stop whirling with the news she was pregnant. Again. With Beckett's child. *Again.*

"What? I don't have the energy to fight with you right now, Beckett. I'm just not—"

He put a hand over her mouth. "I love you."

She shook her head, unsure she'd heard him right. God, how long had she wished to hear those words from this man? Since she'd met him, basically.

"I know we fought the last time we were together. We do that a lot. We're good at it, you and I. Both stubborn and hardheaded. It's why we make such a great team. I had to get everything set up, do what I could to ensure nothing like this would ever happen again to you or Sean. The call from our boy shifted the timeline around, but I'm here, and I'm *not* going anywhere unless it's with you."

He read the question in her eyes and shook his head. "I'm not with EGIS anymore, so don't even go there. Michael was behind a lot."

She nodded. "I know. I checked out something DeSalvo told me. I'll kill the bastard if I see him again."

"Don't give either of them another thought." He dug in his pocket and placed the box in her hand. "This is for you, Iggy."

"What's this?"

"Something I've kept around since that night we were supposed to meet at Snakes."

She opened the top and lost all words as she stared at the ring seated in the box. Princess cut with pear-shaped and pavé accents along the white gold band. With a trembling hand, she withdrew it from the box. Something etched on the inside caught her eye, and she looked closer.

"What's this date?"

"You don't know?"

She thought about it and almost smiled. "This is the date I first started at EGIS."

"The day you walked into my life and stole my heart. I've loved you from that day and will far beyond the time the good Lord sees fit to take me from this earth." He angled her chin so she looked at him. "Marry me, Indigo Grey."

She nodded as she placed her hand on his face. "Yes," she whispered. "Yes, I'll marry you." For so long it had been nothing but a fantasy to imagine Beckett and her together; she wasn't about to run anymore. "I love you, too, Beckett."

He slipped the ring on her finger and kissed her. Only when someone cleared his throat did he pull back from her. Her neighbor stood there with Sean. Moments later, her boy was back in her lap. The doctor came in and filled them all in on what she had to do. Beckett never released her hand, and she didn't want him to.

"I'll have your release papers at the desk." The doctor smiled at them before leaving.

"I need to go home," she muttered.

"*We*," Beckett interjected. "*We* are going home." He slid his arm around Indigo, taking another kiss.

Epilogue

NEARLY THREE YEARS LATER

The deep-throated barks from the dog were the first thing Beckett heard when he stepped from the house onto the porch. The second was the childish squeals of joy. Around the corner of the house Sean appeared, now age ten, holding a leash leading the barking dog. Behind the dog sat his nearly three-year-old daughter, Raina, being pulled in a sled. Trailing both of them came the woman who made his life all the more worthwhile. His wife and the mother of his children. Indigo.

She had dressed in jeans and a yellow sweatshirt with an angel on it, hiking boots on her feet. Her hair floated in silken waves around her shoulders, moving as she did. She turned her head and gave him a wide smile before she put her attention on their daughter, who seemed to be having the ride of her life.

Sean was wonderful with her, determined she wouldn't grow up to be a girly girl, and he made sure to include her when he went out to get dirty. Raina doted on her brother and would follow him anywhere.

Beckett ambled down to the ground. Catching up to them as Raina's ride finished, they released the dog and then headed to the swing set. Munky, the rescued lab mix, named after the T. rex from one of Sean's favorite stories, bounded after them, barking every step of the way.

"Thought you had some consulting to take care of," Indigo said as she turned her face up for his kiss.

"Done."

"Went off easier than expected?"

"It did. In and out."

"Glad to hear it."

Beckett worked for the local police department that occasionally called on him to help with consulting work. Indigo hadn't gone back to work outside the house, not wanting to miss any of their children's growing up. Being hunted by EGIS was no longer a concern—the man who'd taken over had assured them of that. For a while they'd both been edgy and unsure, but as time moved along, nothing changed. Their lives were their own.

And yet, in the back of his mind part of him still wondered if she wasn't worried about them being taken from her again. Not a problem, because he'd always be there to protect his family, and as long as she was happy, so was he.

Readjusting to stand behind her, he wrapped his arms around her and rested his head on her shoulder. She reached up and touched the side of his face.

"Sean told me what Raina wants for her birthday this

year."

"What's that?"

"A brother or sister to play with."

He laughed. "Really? What did you say?"

"Nothing, just kind of grunted."

He nuzzled her neck. "I like it when you grunt." She pushed back against him. "What do you think?"

She turned in his arms and looped her own around his neck. "I think, Papa, she's going to get her wish in about six months or thereabouts."

It took a moment for her words to sink in. He could hardly contain his excitement. "Really?"

Indigo nodded. "I go to the doctor Wednesday. Home test says yes, however. Are you okay with this?"

Hell yes, he was. "Absolutely. I love you, Indigo."

"And I you."

They shared a kiss, and he recalled what Sean had told him the day he'd discovered Beckett was his father. He'd given him the code name Papa. And nothing had ever fit him so well.

Acknowledgments

This wouldn't have happened without Entangled giving me a shot, and so, thank you to the company and editors. I appreciate being allowed to be part of the family.

About the Author

A *USA Today* best-selling author, Aliyah Burke is an avid reader and is never far from pen and paper (or the computer). She loves to hear from her readers and can be reached here. She can also be found on Facebook, Twitter: @AliyahBurke96, or TSU: @AliyahBurke. You can also join her in her yahoo group.

She is married to a career military man. They are owned by three borzoi and a DSH cat. She spends her days sharing time between her work, writing, and dog training. She caps off with some showing, racing, and coursing her dogs, for which they travel all over to enter.